You Were Never Mine

By:

Annissa Gonzales

Table of Contents

PART ONE: *THE INCEPTION* 1

PART TWO: *THE CONNECTION* 76

PART THREE: *THE DECEPTION* 125

First Printing Edition, 2024

All rights are reserved. No part of this book may be reproduced, distributed, or transmitted in any form or by any means, including photocopying, recording, or other electronic or mechanical methods, without the prior written permission of the author, except in the case of brief quotations embodied in critical reviews and certain other noncommercial uses permitted by copyright law.

Library of Congress Control Number: 2024938211
Paperback ISBN: 978-1-963258-36-3
Hardcover ISBN: 978-1-963258-37-0

Printed By:

Book Writing Crew

PART ONE

The Inception

It was a regular night out. We were all going to get together at a bar and have some drinks. Half of the group was out already, they decided to start early while the rest of us stayed back and got ready. It was the first time I had been out with everyone in two or three weeks. It may not seem like that long, but if you knew us you would know that we were inseparable. I was drifting away from them, I had been for a while, but after that night I knew it needed to be done. *Just one more night*, that's all I kept telling myself as I continued to get dressed. I texted Cee to see if she was ready and made my way to pick her up. We had our usual talks on the road and all I kept thinking about was how we used to do this every Friday night. It was girls' night. Dinner, drinks, and dancing. All I ever cared about was seeing *HER* though.

"We're picking up Lisa before we head to the bar," Cee says as I snap back into reality. I couldn't remember the last time I had seen Lisa, I thought to myself. We were never that close, but it would be nice to see her.

We arrived at Lisa's half an hour later and got off to see her new house. Cee had already seen it before, but she wanted me to come in and check it out while she finished getting dressed. Cee and Lisa were talking in the room as I sat in the living room and waited. Cee was closer to Lisa than I was. They were "best friends" which never made any sense to me because Cee had always called HER, her best friend. Anyway, a few minutes later they came out of the room, and we all decided to take a shot or two before heading out. I called Alex a few times, but he never picked up. Cee said he texted her the name of the bar when we were taking off, so we headed that way.

"He's still not answering," I said to Cee as we were pulling up to the bar. We decided to park and go inside anyway. It was a nice little spot. I had never been there before. We make our way around the inside and then out to the back patio trying to find Alex and the rest of the group. After about 15 minutes of circling the place we all agreed to leave. We figured since they started early, and we took forever that they continued without us.

At this point I was ready to call it a night.

"We should go to *Vibe*," Cee said.

"Yes! Let's go, it will be like old times. Just us three," said Lisa. *Vibe* was our go to spot every Friday night after dinner. It was a nice place, with good drinks and a decently sized dance floor. Plus, they always played the best music. That was our favorite thing about it. It was crowded when we arrived, as we got there late. We made our way over to the bar to grab a couple drinks and since we were all sober, we decided to grab a table outside. We sat around the table, catching up with one another when Alex called. He said everyone was pretty much wasted and they had decided to make their way back home.

"Ooh, I love this song! Come on ladies, let's go dance," Cee said, disregarding Alex's call. I told them to go on without me, I just wasn't in the mood just yet. They went in and I stayed outside and pulled out my phone. I scrolled through social media while the girls were inside, passing time while they danced when I came across a certain post. *Avery*, I saw to myself as I stared at the picture. It was a picture of her and a few other people, whom I'm assuming were some of her friends. It looked like they had been drinking. *Why did that catch my attention?*

I continue to scroll through my feed and come across another post of hers. It was a video of them taking shots and I couldn't help but laugh at the face she made at the end. I'm not sure what possessed me to message her. Boredom, I assume, but I type something out anyway. We sent a few meaningless messages back and forth before the girls came back and I put my phone away. We decided we would stay for two more rounds and then we would call it a night. On the way to drop off Lisa I pulled out my phone and sent Avery another message.

"What are your plans for the rest of the night?" I type out. No, not that.

"We should hang out." No, that's too straight forward.

"What are you up to?" Yeah, that's not too bad. I hit send. She responds back instantly. I honestly was not expecting it, but I opened it anyway.

"I'm about to head home. I was out of town," she said.

"I'm headed home too," I replied. "If you're not tired, you should stop by for a drink. You can bring your friends if you want." That was bold of me, but hopefully the "friends" comment will ease the invite. Cee's phone rings.

"Alex is calling, I bet he wants us to go over." She answered the phone and Alex let us know he was with another friend or ours and they were going to be hanging out if we wanted to stop by. Cee sounds very excited about going. I agreed, even though I made plans because Avery still had not responded. I didn't get too hung up on it though. We had never actually hung out before. Not without Ivan.

Ivan was my best friend. We had known each other for years. He walked in the first day of our second semester sophomore year. When our teacher finished his introduction, he asked Ivan to pick and empty seat. I watched as some of the girls blushed, trying to make room for him, and to my surprise, he made his way towards me. He walked up to my table and pointed towards the chair.

"Hey, uhm, do you mind?" he asked quietly. I moved my things and watched as he took his seat.

"I'm Chloe," I say quietly to which he smiled. We were inseparable ever since that first day. Avery was his girlfriend.

We were about fifteen minutes from home when I saw my phone light up. I checked it, thinking it was Alex since Cee's phone had died. It was Avery. *Oh shit, she messaged me back.*

"Is it Alex?" Cee asked. "Tell him we're almost there," she said.

"It's not Alex, but I'll let him know." I stare at my phone for a second before I open the message.

"I'm not with friends. I was with my sisters and my cousins. I can stop by though, let me know when you're home." I'm not sure how to respond. I didn't think she would agree to come. Maybe she'll pick up Ivan and they will both come over. What if he wonders why I invited her and didn't tell him? No, he wouldn't think it's weird. He's always wanted us to be friends. Of course, he did. I was his best friend, and she was his girlfriend. I'm thinking this through way too hard. "Okay, sounds good. I'm almost home." I replied.

We pull into town and head straight to Alex. We didn't bother stopping for drinks because Alex always had some ready for us. He was good about that. On the way there I mentioned to Cee that I had made plans before Alex called and invited us over.

"Why didn't you tell me?" Cee asked.

"You never want to hang out with us anymore." We pulled up to the house and I let Cee know that I would get off and say hi and then I was leaving. We made our way up the driveway, and everyone was outside. As we're walking up, I slightly stop, trying not to make it noticeable as I see HER. *Dammit*, I think to myself, but continue walking. I greet everyone and walk up to Alex to let him know I'm leaving.

"I didn't know she was going to be here. I didn't even know she would be in town." Alex said.

"It's fine," I say. "I have other plans. I was just coming to say bye."

"Don't be like that. Hey! Hold on a second." Alex yells out as I continue to make my way back to the car. I head back home and grab a drink. I was glad I left. There was no way I would have made it through the rest of the night with her there. Shit. I forgot to message Avery. I pulled out my phone and typed out a quick text.

"Hey, I know it's late, but I'm home now if you still want to come by." I hit send knowing she probably wouldn't respond. I look to see if there's any kind of drink I could make her, just in case. I hear my phone go off. She's here.

I, for some odd reason, check myself in the mirror and stop and think *what the fuck am I doing*? I walked over to the front door to let her in. To my surprise, she's alone. She comes in and I offer her a drink. We headed over to the living room. I play some music and we start talking. I ask her about Ivan, trying not to make it awkward, and she tells me they had a fight and are not talking at the moment. That's why she had been out with her family, to get her mind off things.

I ask if she wants to talk about it as she takes a sip of her drink and says, "All I want is this." We continued to talk and drink and talk a little more and drink a little more. I realized I had never actually talked to her like this before. We took a trip several months prior to this as a group, but other than the small talk I made with her around Ivan, this was the first time. We had drinks one night too, but I was involved with HER, so I never paid any attention to Avery.

As we continued to talk and laugh, I noticed that anytime I would look at her, she would begin to blush. Stop, I think to myself. *Not this one, she's with Ivan.* The more I continued to try to avoid it, the more I continued to notice it. I get up to get us another drink and she follows me to the kitchen. She was sitting at the table when I turned around, just watching me.

"You like what you see?" I ask and freeze instantly. *Why the hell did I say that*?

"Can I get some more ice?" she asked.

As I turn back toward the fridge, I hear her say "I do like what I see." *There it is. That's exactly what I was waiting for.* I turned around to face her, smile lightly, and we headed back into the living room. I decide to test the waters, making little sly remarks just to see her reaction, and to my surprise, she throws them right back. The last time I got to grab a beer I watched her eyes follow me out of the room. While in the kitchen I thought to myself, *am I really going to do this? She's Ivans girlfriend…but they're not together*. I walked back into the living room and as she watched me make my way to the couch I said, "are you just going to keep staring, or are you going to do something about it?" She kept her eyes on mine as she inched closer towards me. I slowly placed my drink down, my eyes never leaving hers. She hesitated before she put her mouth on mine. I stayed perfectly still, letting her take her time. She kissed me softly, and it took everything in me not to pin her to the couch. She pulled back slightly, just enough that I noticed the change in her breathing. She grabbed my hand and led me away from the couch and into my bedroom. I pulled my shirt off as I made my way to the bed. I reached for my shorts, and she pulled my arms away.

  I looked up at her, immediately thinking I had the wrong idea. "Let me," she said. She pushed me back onto the bed and climbed on top. I watched her as I let her hands run up and down my body, and soon after, she allowed her mouth to do the same. The slowness of it all was beginning to drive me crazy. I went to flip her on her back, but quickly, she pinned me down. "Stay still, let me please you."

  I sat at my desk the following Monday unable to concentrate on any of my work. Flashbacks of the other night were currently on replay in my head. *Avery, Avery, why am I thinking about Avery? Better questions, how did I never notice her? Could I not see her because of Ivan? Did my friendship with him cause me to naturally just block her out? If so, what changed?* Avery was… alluring, to say the least. I think about how shy and almost unsure she was that night. And how in an instance, she was confident, knowing exactly what she wanted. She was intriguing and every part of me wanted more. Not only did I want her body, but I wanted to take a deep dive into her mind. As much as I wanted this, I had to let her come to me. Was I letting my pride get in the way? Oh definitely, but my ego would thank me later. Wednesday afternoon, I received a text. I pull my phone from my desk and see her name across the screen. Sooner than I expected.

"Sorry to bother you, you're probably working. What was the drink you made me the other night? I've had a long day and really need something to relax." *Should I invite her over? I could make her one after work.. She's obviously being thing about the other night too. I need to be smart with this one.* I'll let it play out for now. I send a quick response and place my phone back in the drawer. I hear a text come through a few minutes later but I choose not to answer. Okay Chloe, focus. The afternoon passes quickly and I gather my things to leave for the evening. I read Avery's message as I make my way to my car.

"Great, thanks! Maybe you could stop by for one after work." I smile and two my phone in my bag. As much as I want to jump at the opportunity, I think it would be better if we both wait a little longer. It will make the next time all the more enjoyable.

The days went by, and I continued to receive messages from Avery. They weren't daily but I was genuinely surprised at the consistency. A part of me wondered how the fact that I didn't respond to the first time would affect how we move on from here. One day while at work I received a text from Ivan.

"The Draft is on tonight. We have to watch it. I'll stop by after work and bring some beer." Football was always our thing. We watched every game together since we went for the same team.

"Sounds good to me. I'll see you after work." I replied. I get home a few hours later and clean up a bit before he comes over. I hadn't seen him in a while, so I was excited for him to stop by. It was a little after six when he arrived. I figured it would take him a while, anyway, just getting out of work and all. He walks in the door with a twelve pack and a couple of tall boys. *Mike's hard lemonade*? I see through the bag. *Why the hell did he bring those*? He puts them in the fridge, brings us a round and sits down and grabs the remote. I've always loved how comfortable he was here. He always made himself at home. I open my beer and we discuss our days at work as we wait for the draft to start. "Oh shit," he says. "I forgot my phone at home. Can you text Avery for me? I told her I would watch the draft here and that she could come by. That's cool with you, right?" he says. *Shit. She's coming. I imagined the next time we saw each other would have been at night. Alone. No clothes. And certainly, no Ivan*!

"Oh yea, of course. I'll text her right now." I haven't seen Avery since the night she was here. That's who the other drinks are for, that makes sense. I really hope this isn't weird, especially since we were going to be drinking. This should be interesting. I pulled out my phone and sent her a text.

"Hey, Ivan just got here. He left his phone at home and wanted me to let you know."

She responded quickly. "Of course, he did. Tell him I'm at my sister's game right now, but I'll stop by after."

Another message comes through. "Did he get my drinks? I'm going to need one for sure." *Why would she need one? Are they fighting again? What if she needs a drink because it's going to be weird being around both of us? I wonder if he knows she was here the other night.* "What did she say?" Ivan asks, interrupting my thoughts.

"She's at her sister's game. She said she would be here afterwards. I told her you got her drinks. She was glad." I said.

"Yeah. She's been in a mood lately, and said she needed a drink. It has nothing to do with us though, just family stuff," he says. *Oh, thank God*, I think to myself and sit back and relax. The draft starts and we sit discussing all the players we want, who we could possibly get and our hopes for the new season. The front door opens and Avery walks in. She says a quick hello and makes her way into the kitchen. I switch seats so she and Ivan can sit together and make myself comfortable. She walks back to the living room with a drink in her hand and a confused look on her face.

"Why did you move? I would have sat on the other couch," she says.

"Shut up babe. Did your sister win her game?" Ivan asked and I was glad I didn't have to respond. They conversed about her day for just a bit before she cut him off and told him to watch the draft. I felt her glance over at me a few times before she made conversation. It was small talk, I tried not to give her too much attention and continued watching T.V. I got up to get a drink, asking if anyone wanted another round, then made my way to the kitchen. I watched my phone light up as I sat back down. It was Avery. I tried not to make any kind of expression as I opened the message, because I could tell she was watching me.

"Your ass looks great in those shorts." I read and tried not to laugh.

Another message comes through "Could you get me some more ice?" I try to keep my composure while reading the message. I carefully looked over at her to meet her gaze, smile and put my phone back down. *She's brave. Maybe this could be fun after all.* We shared a few flirtatious glances back and forth, trying not to make it noticeable and then I heard her speak.

"Oh, I forgot. I need to show you something." I didn't look at her, thinking she was talking to Ivan.

"Chloe," she says, and I look over at her. "I have to show you something. Come here." She gets up and walks towards the room. I look over at Ivan as I follow her. He shrugs and turns his attention back towards the T.V. We walked into my room, and she shut the door. "What the hell are you doing?" I ask. She takes a step towards me and reaches for the bottom of my shirt.

"Surprised to see me?" she asked. "I would of preferred a different scenario. You know, you naked… and no Ivan," I say as I rep my shirt off. She smiled.

"And I would have preferred this sooner," she said as her mouth met mine. I let her hands roam over my body feverently before I stopped her. She stared at me in disbelief as I bent down to get my shirt. I kissed her quickly.

"Let's go. I'm sure he is waiting for us," I say and walk back into the living room. We continue to watch the draft and at this point I can no longer focus. *Did she really just do that? Is this going to be a problem now?* I could stop this, but every part of me tells me not to. This is going to be fun.

This was definitely one of the more challenging hook ups I've ever had. Women have always been fun to me, but that's all it was. Though, romantically I prefer men, being sexual with a woman gave me something I could never get from a man. Having a woman worship every inch of your body was gratifying and I was addicted to the feeling. But I avoided emotional attachment to warn at all cost. I was not equipped to handle women emotionally, so I made it a point to only sleep with women who were in relationships with men. That way at least I knew they had someone to dump all their feelings on. Now, I'm not monster, trust. Before starting something with any woman, I was sure to advise them on how I do things. They were to walk away at any time, but I'd be damned if a woman held me accountable for her own attachment issues. Although, it has happened once or twice.

I began seeing a lot more of Avery, and not just for sex. I wanted to know everything about her. It started with the occasional dinner and drinks, usually if one of us had a long day, or just needed to vent. I learned in that time that she enjoyed long car rides, preferably at night. The darkness allowed her to speak of things that she's never been able to say out loud, and my calmness kept her comfortable. Late night talks turning into pillow talk and after hours of her letting me explore her mind, id give her house of exploring my body, though it never seemed like enough. One night, while laying in bed, I could tell something was bothering her. I turned over, leaning up on one arm and brushed her hair out of her face.

"Avery, are you okay?" I asked softly.

Without hesitation she looked up at me and said, "I feel like I don't know you. Lately I feel like I've just been laying naked in a stranger's bed." *There it is*. I let out a deep breath.

"What do you want to know?" I ask.

"Anything," she said excitingly, and I laugh.

"Uhm, I don't know what to say. I'm not much of a talker," I say. The excitement in her eyes quickly faded.

"Chloe, come on. You can talk to Iv.."

"Woah, no! I would appreciate it if we could not mention his name while naked. Please," I say slightly disgusted.

"Well, maybe you should put a shirt on, because there's something I need to tell you," she said.

My heart was racing. What could she possibly need to say. I got out of bed and there on an oversized shirt. She sat at the edge of the bed as I leaned against the dresses. I was becoming fidgety. *Why am I so nervous?*

"Ivan got a new job. I think we're going to move." I stayed quiet. I started wondering what that would mean for us. I mean, we weren't together, she was not my girlfriend, but she had easily become the closest person to me.

"Did you hear me?" she asked.

"What? Sorry, yes. He hasn't mentioned anything to me," I said. "He got the call a couple of days ago. I think he already found a place." "They're leaving," I whisper to myself.

"Sorry, I didn't hear you," she said.

"Oh, nothing. Are you excited?" I ask, trying to focus.

"I guess," she says. "I won't have to drive back and forth anymore. We'll be moving over there."

Avery worked forty-five minutes away from the small town we live in. *He must have been planning this for a while now, so it would be easier for her. He really does love her. Anyone could see that.* "You could come stay the weekend with us." she says excitedly. Before even thinking I say "no."

She looks at me confused. "You're moving Avery. It's serious now. He's trying to build a future with you. I can't be there all the time," I said.

"You're his best friend! Of course, he's going to want you there…and so will I," she says as she reaches out to grab my hand.

"I should probably take you home now. The sun's about to come up," I say as I attempt to pull away.

She pulls me back in, "He knows I'm here." I turn and look at her.

"Besides, he has to work today. I told him I was staying with you when I left last night." I smile,

"Then let's go to sleep," and we laugh.

It was early afternoon when I woke up. My arm felt numb and when I finally opened my eyes, I realized she was lying on me, and I had one arm wrapped around her. I couldn't remember the last time I slept this well, even though it was just for a few hours. I looked down at Avery and admired how peaceful she looked in that moment. I slowly rubbed my finger against her cheek, trying not to wake her. *What am I doing? Stop.* I remove my arm and quietly get out of bed. Just as I was grabbing clothes out of my dresser, I hear her say "Good morning."

"Hi," I said quietly.

"What's wrong?" she asked.

"Oh, nothing," I say. "We better get up."

I'm lost in a trance when I hear her walk into the bathroom. "Are you okay?" she asked.

"Yeah, I'm good," I say.

"I forgot I made plans with Alex and the group tonight." *Why the hell am I lying?*

"Ivan will probably be getting home shortly anyway. I'll take you back." We drive in silence on the way to their house. I glance over at her, and she looks deep in thought. I pulled up in the driveway and put the car in park.

"Thanks for staying with me. It was fun," I say. She looks like she's going to say something, but just smiles and gets out of the car.

I get in the shower as soon as I get home, trying not to over analyze the situation. When I'm out I check my phone. There were no new messages. *Did I really think she would message me? Maybe she's upset.* I go to send her a message, but instead I text Alex to see what he's up to. A few minutes later my phone rang, and my heart stopped. *Shit, what if it's her.*

It was Alex. "Hey! Get dressed, we're going out. I'll pick you up in an hour," he says. So that's what I do. I turn some music on, find an outfit and start to get dressed. I go to the fridge and grab a beer, deciding to get an early start. It was a little after seven when Alex texted. "Change of plans, we're drinking at my house. Come by when you're ready." I headed back into my room and tried to find a different outfit. I go for something more casual since we're staying in. I threw on some shorts and a shirt and let Alex know I was on my way. I recognize most of the cars when I'm pulling up and let him know I'm outside. He comes out to greet me as he always does and gives me a big hug.

"Everyone is going to be excited to see you," he says.

"Come on, let's go inside." We walk in the door, and he yells out "look who's here!" Everyone turns to face us.

"Oh my gosh! Chloe! You're here." said one of the girls and a few of the others make their way over to say hi. I make my way around the room when I hear a familiar voice.

"Hey Chlo," I hear and stop immediately. I turn around and meet her gaze. A sudden chill runs down my spine. It was HER. "Hey," I say.

"Here, I grabbed you a beer," she said. I reach out to grab it and turn to walk away, but she begins to speak again.

"How have you been?" she asked. I'm not in the mood for small talk, especially with HER.

"I'm great," I say, and walk away. Throughout the night everyone makes their way up to me with the same questions.

"Where have you been? How have you been?" and the usual "You know, we really miss you around here. It hasn't been that long," I finally said to one of the girls.

"It's been three months Chloe." It's that familiar voice again. I look over at HER and there's an awkward moment of silence.

"Well, she's back now. So, let's party!" Alex exclaims and we all laugh and get back to drinking. I feel my phone buzz in my back pocket and take it out. Woah, I'm a little tipsier than I thought I was. I try to focus on the screen and see Ivans name. I watched it ring, not sure why I was hesitant on answering. I waited a few minutes before I called him back. I was standing in the kitchen when he answered. I could barely hear him over the music.

"What's up?" I say when he answers the call.

"Hey! We're going to cook out tomorrow so come by." he says and before I can respond he says "Wait, are you at a party?" I laugh. "Yeah, I'm at Alex's. I'll be there tomorrow though."

"Okay. Be safe. Don't drink too much, save some energy for Sunday funday," he says.

"Who are you yelling at?" I hear Avery's voice in the background.

"Chloe. She's at Alex's getting drunk. She can't hear me." We both laugh.

"Is she..." I heard her start to say something and before she could finish, I say I have to go, and I'll see them tomorrow and hang up. I turned to head back to the living room and saw HER standing in the doorway.

"How long are you going to stay mad at me?" she asks. *Here we go again*. I knew the minute she got drunk she was going to start this. "I'm not mad at you. I just don't care to be around you," I say as I walk past her.

"I didn't mean any of those things I said," she yells out at me. "How many times do I have to say sorry?" Everyone was staring at us.

We had a big fight the last time we were together, and everyone saw us. I'm sure that's why they were all staring. They were all probably thinking the same thing as I was. *Here we go again*. We spent a lot of time together the past couple of years. Some days were good, some days were bad, but towards the end it was terrible all the time. I had a boyfriend when we met and so did she. He knew I was into women, that never bothered him. As long as he knew what was going on, it was fine. Her boyfriend, on the other hand, didn't know about her. He always assumed it though, and he wasn't a fan. They fought a lot about it. Especially when me and my boyfriend decided to end things. We started hanging out more. We would always joke that I left him for her, which was not the case at all. We just had different plans for our future and though we loved each other, knew it would work out in the long run. It was not an ugly breakup, nor was it a sad one. She used it to her advantage though and would say I was sad and needed a friend as an excuse to hang out more. One night, when we were drinking, she told me she loved me. I never said it back. That's when the fights began. I explained to her time and time again that I didn't date women. Though it sounds wrong, and seems unfair, women were just fun to me, and it would never become more than that. I should have stopped then, but I didn't. It was easy being with HER. I knew if I ever wanted to hook up that she would be okay with it, and at the end of the day we were friends anyway. I never paid attention to the hurt it was causing her. One day though, it just became too much for her. We were drinking at Alex's that night, and Alex and I were talking on the back porch. We had recently begun seeing each other, nothing serious, just a few dates, but we haven't told anyone yet. We wanted to make sure it worked before we got everyone else involved. I was giving him a quick kiss before going back inside when I saw HER standing at the window. She had been watching us the whole time. She opened the back door and stared at us. Her face mixed with both sadness and anger.

"What the hell is going on?" she asked.

"Are the two of you together now or something?"

"No," I say and look over at Alex. "We've gone on a few dates, but we haven't told anyone." She looked over at Alex and he put his head down. She turned her attention back to me. Alex tried to speak, and she put her hand up and walked inside. After a few more drinks she became angrier, and at the end of the night she blew up on me.

"You're a horrible person, you know that right? You only think about yourself!" she yelled out. Everyone stopped what they were doing and looked at us.

"You can't just go around messing with people's feelings. I tell you I love you and what do you do? You decide I'm not good enough and go and get with Alex?" The room had fallen silent. All eyes were focused on us. I look over at Alex and then back to HER.

"I should go," I say and walk into the kitchen to grab my things. She starts yelling again as soon as I walk away, but I pay her no attention. I was becoming frustrated and didn't want to say anything I didn't mean since I had been drinking. I walked out the door and she followed me to the car. Alex was not far behind her, but he waited on the front porch.

"You're not even going to say anything? You're just going to leave?" she asked, and I finally snapped.

"That's enough!" I yell out and she freezes.

"You knew exactly what this was when we started, and I reminded you time and time again. You chose to stick around anyway, so stop playing victim. I'm sick of this already, and I'm sick of you." I opened my car door and she just stood there watching me, tears running down her face. I look over at Alex and drive away. Tonight was the first time we had been face to face since then.

"I should go," I said, everyone was still watching us. I head out the door and Alex follows me outside.

"This was a bad idea," I say to him, and we walk towards my car. "You should have told me she was going to be here."

"I guess I figured after all this time she would let it go," he says. "I'm sorry."

"Yeah, me too. Tell everyone I said bye. Enjoy the rest of your night," I say, and get in my car and drive off. I got home and changed my clothes. I went into the kitchen to grab a glass of water. By this time the alcohol had worn off and I was ready for bed. I was staring up at the ceiling thinking about the events of tonight. *Gosh, that was such a mess.*

I start to think about Avery and our whole situation. I don't want us to end up like that. She's a good person, and she has become an even better friend over time. Maybe the move will be a good thing after all. Less time spent together, less time fooling around. We can talk about it tomorrow. *Oh shit, the cookout. I better get some sleep.* It's a little after one when I head to the store to grab a few things before heading over to Ivan's. It's beautiful outside, and I wasn't in the mood for beer, so I grabbed some juice to make us mixed drinks. I brought over a bottle of Malibu since it's not too strong. It's also Sunday and we all have to go to work tomorrow. No need to get too crazy. I pull up the driveway and see a couple of cars already there. *Oh, we're having a party.* I let myself in, as I always do, Ivan hates when I knock.

"My house is your house" he always says. It's quiet when I walk in, everyone must be in the back... I walk into the kitchen and see Avery standing in front of the sink. She is staring out of the window, and I can't tell if she's staring at something or if she's thinking.

"Hey," I say as I open the fridge. She jumps and I laugh.

"Sorry, I didn't mean to scare you. I wasn't sure if you were deep in thought or admiring Ivan at the grill," I say jokingly. She stares at me and rolls her eyes. I walk over to the cabinet to grab two glasses.

"Are you just going to stare, or did you want to say something?" I ask. She opens her mouth, but no words come out. I make us both a drink while she stands there.

"Here," I say, handing her a drink. "Now stop being weird, I'm going outside to say my hello's." I walk outside and Ivan introduces me to the two couples sitting around the table. He works with both guys at the shop and had invited them over for drinks. I've never seen him hang out with any of his co-workers. *He must have invited them over to tell them the big news.* That's such an Ivan thing to do. Invite people over, watch them all have a good time, knowing he wouldn't have to do this again because he was leaving.

"Was Avery in there when you came in?" he asked.

"Yeah, I made her a drink. I'll head back in and see if she needs help with anything," I say, and make my way back inside. She's still standing at the sink when I walk in, this time with her back facing the window. She looks up at me and then back down at her drink.

"Alright, what is it?" I ask and take a seat at the table. "Avery, at least come sit down." After a minute or two she walks over to the table. I place my hand on her arm when she sits down. "What's wrong?" I ask. I saw Ivan coming towards the door and I pulled my hand away quickly. She gives me a look, like she can't believe I just did that and keeps looking at me as Ivan approaches the table.

"What's up?" he asks and sets his hand on her shoulder. She rolls her eyes.

"Trying to figure out what sides we should make," I say, and she scoffs. He doesn't notice.

"Just make potato salad. I'm going to throw some corn on the grill so that will be good enough," he says.

"Come outside when you finish. It's nice out there." He gives Avery's shoulder a quick squeeze and goes back outside.

"Are the two of you fighting again?" I ask. She says nothing. I get up and start getting the pot ready for the potatoes.

"We're not fighting," she says as she walks over to help. "I don't think I want to go," she says quietly. I stop peeling and look at her. She puts her knife down and looks at me.

"It's just all happening so fast and I'm not sure I'm ready. My life is here, my family, my friends…and you," she stops.

"Yeah, about that," I say. "We should talk."

We finished the potatoes, put them to boil and sat down at the table. "Look Avery," I say, and I can already tell she's over the conversation.

"Whether you go, or decide to stay, this thing between us has to stop. You're very important to me, Avery. This friendship that we've built has easily become one that I can't lose. And Ivan," she stops me.

"Do not use him as an excuse. That has never stopped you before. If you don't want this anymore that's fine, but come up with a better reason than Ivan," she says.

"It's not an excuse," I start to say, and she stops me again. "I want to know the real reason, not something you just made up to make me feel better," she says. I just stared at her. She completely caught me off guard.

"I just don't want you thinking this is more than what it is. I don't want the hooking up to ruin our friendship. I know how messy it can get and I don't want you to hate me." She was quiet for a moment and then she laughed.

Now I was the one looking confused. "Let me get this straight," she pauses.

"You think because I had my arm around you that I was catching feelings for you?" she asks, still laughing. I was not expecting her to say that. "Yeah, I felt you move my arm and get out of bed. And then, you went out to drink because you didn't know what to do or what to say." I smile. *She knows me so well*. We both start laughing, and when we finally calm down, it's her who rests her hand on my arm.

"Listen to me," she says. "I'm a big girl, okay? If I ever catch myself developing any kind of feeling for you, I will let you know. I promise." She holds out her pinky. I smile and hook mine into hers.

"Oh, and one more thing," she says as she leans towards me. "Don't act like this is all on me." She places her hand gently against my cheek.

"I think we started our day a little like this, right?" she asked as she mimics the way I ran my finger against her cheek.

"I think you're getting soft Chloe," I put my head down and laughed. We finish up in the kitchen and head outside. We were all sitting around talking while Ivan finished up the food and went back inside to eat. The food was great. After we finish, we continue with our drinks and converse a little more. I got up to start cleaning, so Ivan and Avery don't have to worry about it later.

"Chloe, come over here." I heard Ivan say and walked back to the table.

"I have news," he says as he stands next to Avery. She hits my leg under the table and gives me a look. *Oh, he's about to break the big news.*

"I got a new job offer," he says and his co-workers trade glances at each other.

"I accepted it," he continues. "It's in another town, about an hour away. We've already found a house too. We leave in a few weeks." I try my hardest to act surprised. Luckily, his co-workers react before I do. They congratulated him on the job and the move. He looks over at me and it hits me. *This is actually happening.* I've been so caught up in everything else that I really hadn't stopped to process the move. We give each other a look that only we understand. A "we'll talk later" kind of look and nod at each other. We continued with our night, played some music, and enjoyed the evening. I was looking for my phone and went over to the kitchen counter to see if I had set it down there. I found it and checked to see if I had any notifications. Two missed calls from Alex and one from a blocked caller. *That had to be HER.* There were a couple of texts from Alex as well.

"Chloe, can we talk?" and "Don't do this, please answer me."

"Is everything okay?" I hear Avery ask and I turn to look at her. "Yeah," I say, and place my phone in my pocket. "I think everyone is getting ready to leave," she says.

"Ivan asked me to come get you." I watch her leave the room before pulling my phone back out.

"I'll call in a bit, okay?" I send back to Alex. Everyone is saying their goodbyes, and the guys congratulate Ivan again. Ivan and I sit outside, enjoying the cool night breeze.

"I'm proud of you," I say, and look over at him.

"You know we're still going to be close right? You can come over whenever you want, hell you can stay over every weekend. Football season is coming up anyway. You know we can't miss a game," he says. I smile at him.

"I'd love that," I say. "It'll be your home away from home," he says. We stayed outside a little while longer before I headed out. I still needed to call Alex.

I didn't talk to Avery or Ivan much over the next two weeks as they were busy getting things ready for the move. Avery decided to go after all. Even though we discussed the situation at the cookout, I still felt like distance was the best thing for us, but I wouldn't tell her that. I enjoyed the time I had spent with Avery. Maybe a little more than I should have. This was all so new to me, still I've never wanted to be around a woman I was sleeping with the way I wanted to be around Avery. I was hoping the distance would give me time to process what's been happening, and what I've been feeling.

I had agreed to have dinner with Alex one evening. It wasn't fair that I had been shutting him out over this whole thing with me and HER, he did nothing wrong. He apologized over and over, and I finally had to tell him to shut up. I told him I would never make him choose between being friends with me or being friends with HER. We finished our meals, but still stayed at the restaurants to have another drink.

"Your birthday is coming up," he says. I wince at the thought. I've never been a fan of celebrating my birthday.

"I don't want to do anything," I say. "Too bad, I'm throwing you a party," he says. "No, please..." I say before he cuts me off.

"You just have to act surprised because I've already invited everyone." I scowl at him as he sits there with his cheesy smile, and I finally gave in.

"You do throw the best parties," I say and his face lights up. *He's more excited than I am, and it's not even his day.* My birthday lands on a Friday and I decided to take the day off. *Why not make it a three-day weekend*? I woke up early that morning already slightly dreading the day. I do want to get my nails done and a new outfit for the party. Alex made the party for Saturday night, just in case I had plans already. I didn't, but it was nice of him anyway. My phone rang, it was Ivan. I answered quickly.

"Helloooo," I say cheerfully. He's already singing happy birthday in the same quirky way as he's always done when I answer. I let him finish, of course, and he started laughing with me.

"I have bad news," he says after we catch our breath.

"Oh, great. Just ruin my day before it even starts," I say.

"Oh, shut up," he says, and we laugh again.

"I'm not going to make it over there this weekend. I have to work. I'm sorry." I stayed quiet for a minute. We've celebrated my birthday together for the past twelve years since we met.

"I'll make it up to you, I promise," he says.

"Okay," I say, trying not to sound upset.

"I have to get back to work. Go enjoy your day," he says, and we hang up. I roll out of bed after a while and get ready for the day. I'm just getting out of the shower when I hear a knock at the front door. *Who the hell could that be*? I go over to open the door.

"Surprise!" she yells out and I almost scream. It was Avery. I stared at her in disbelief.

"Happy birthday. I brought breakfast," she says. I just stand there, still in shock.

"Here," she says, handing me the bag.

"Take this inside." I watch her as she walks back to her car. She pops the trunk open and pulls out her suitcase.

"I'm staying with you for the weekend," she says as she walks past me and into the kitchen. I followed her and set the food down on the table.

"What are you doing here?" I say, having a late reaction.

"Sorry, that sounded rude." She stops me.

"It's fine," she says. "Ivan and I were talking earlier this week, and your birthday came up. He felt bad because he was going to miss it and I figured this was the perfect opportunity to come see you." I was still in shock.

"Maybe I should have called first?" she asks nervously. It was then that I realized I was still looking at her confused.

"No. Sorry," I say laughing. "I'm glad you're here. Really. I'm just surprised." I look at her and smile.

She relaxes again. "Should we eat?" I ask. She smiles and pulls out our food.

We're sitting at the nail salon, getting pedicures, and talking about what we're going to do for the rest of the day.

"Oh, by the way, Alex is throwing me a surprise party tomorrow night," I say.

"Why? You hate surprises," she says.

"And yet, here you are," I say jokingly. She rolls her eyes at me. "I can go stay with my parents if you want. I don't want to intrude on your plans more than I already have," she says.

"I'm telling you because I want you to come with me," I say. "You came to spend my birthday with me, didn't you?" She's never met my friends, and I can tell she's overthinking the whole thing. I reached over and give her arm a slight squeeze, trying to bring her back to reality.

"I want you there," I say.

"It'll be fun." She lets out a deep breath.

"I guess we'll have to go shopping then, won't we?" she says. I can tell she's trying to act excited, but I can still tell she's questioning it. "Can we nap before we go?" I ask as we're leaving the salon.

"Really?" she asks.

"It's your birthday and you want to take a nap?" Now it was me who was rolling my eyes.

"It's my birthday, and I want nothing more than to go home, lay on my bed and take a nap." She laughs.

"Okay," she says.

"You're getting old." she teases, and we make our way back to the house. I open the front door and head straight to my room and flop down on the bed.

"Scoot over," she laughs and proceeds to do the same. We talked for a bit, and I fell asleep. When I wake up, I'm alone. I sat up and looked around the room and grabbed my phone. *Damn, I overslept.*

"Avery?" I called out, no response. I walk out of the room and around the house.

"Avery?" I called out again.

"In here," she says, and I head towards the kitchen. I grab a glass of water and watch her as she sits at the table on her laptop. She looks focused. I noticed that she's changed and already dressed. Before I can say anything, she begins to speak.

"Go get dressed. Wear something nice, I made dinner reservations," she says.

"I thought you wanted to go shopping?" I say as I walk over to the table. She looks up at me, I think she's upset.

"I already went," she says.

"You looked comfortable. I didn't want to wake you up. So, I went by myself." I put my head down.

"I'm sorry, Avery. You should have woken me up. I would have gone with you," I say.

"It's fine," she says and closes her laptop. "Besides, I didn't get you a present. So, it was the perfect chance to get you something. Oh, and I got you an outfit too."

"You got me an outfit?" I asked, confused.

"Yeah, for your party tomorrow. Don't worry, it's black. You'll love it," she says, and I laugh. I go back to my room and try to find something nice to wear for dinner. I hear my phone going off somewhere under the blankets, but don't get to it time to answer.

"No Caller ID" it had to be HER. She had to be calling for my birthday, and because she heard about the party. I toss my phone back on the bed and try to find something to wear.

"How nice do I need to look?" I call out to Avery. I pull out a maroon dress from the closet as I wait for an answer. "I like that one," she says from behind me, and I jump.

"Why do you do that?" I ask as I try to catch my breath.

"Do what?" she asks laughing. I threw a pillow at her, grabbed my dress, and ran to the bathroom. I stand at the sink and attempt to do my hair. I go for a wavy look and pull it up halfway. May makeup is still done from this morning, just needs a little touching up. I slipped into my dress and walked back to my room to find some shoes. Avery's laying back on the bed when I walk in and sits up instantly. She eyes me intensely.

"What?" I ask.

"Does it look bad?" I turn to face the mirror. I can see her still looking at me and I turn around to face her.

"Hello," I say.

"Does it look okay?" I ask. She finally speaks. "You look stunning," she says shyly and turns away. *She's blushing.*

"Help me pick out some shoes so we can go," I say. "I'm starving."

She drives as we make our way to the restaurant.

"Where are we going anyway?" I ask. She smiles at me.

"You'll see," she says. I stare out of the window and suddenly begin to feel nervous. *It's just dinner and it's just Avery. I saw the way she looked at me. She's going to be here all weekend. I told myself I wasn't going to do this anymore. It's way easier to say when she's not right next to me.* I snap out of it as we're pulling up to the restaurant. My eyes light up and I can see her smiling at me.

"Oh my gosh. I love this place!" I say, smiling from ear to ear. "Ivan told me about it when we were talking about me coming to stay for the weekend.," she says. It was this nice little Italian place that opened just a few years ago and I loved it. Ivan and I went to try it out when it first opened.

"This feels like a couple's restaurant," he said when we first went there. It had dim lighting and didn't have tables big enough for more than four people. I thought it was cute but could see why he called it that. "I've never been here before," she says as she parks the car.

"Ivan has never brought you here?" I ask as I check my reflection in the mirror.

"You know that man hates being out in public," she says, sounding annoyed at the thought. I laugh.

"Well allow me to introduce you to your new favorite restaurant," I said excitedly, and we got out of the car.

"Reservation for Avery," she tells the older gentleman at the front when we walk in. I watch her as we walk through the restaurants as she takes it all in. We're seated in a round booth towards the back and we scoot in.

"Wow," she says quietly.

"This place is really nice."

"Ivan always says it looks like a couple's restaurant," I say and suddenly become nervous. She gives me a puzzled look and laughs.

"A couple's restaurant?" she asks, still laughing.

"Yeah," I say, laughing too.

"He said the dim light and the way they have the tables set up makes it look like it's for couples."

She looks around. "I guess I could see that," she says. The waiter starts walking our way. He's a nice-looking guy, about 6"1 and a great smile. "Ladies," he says, flashing that smile.

"Welcome." He keeps his eyes on me, and I look away shyly. "What can I start you off with tonight?" he asks.

"We'll take a bottle of Moscato. Chilled." Avery says before I can get a word out.

He nods his head. "Moscato, great choice. What are we celebrating?" he asks and looks down at me again.

Avery places her hand on mine, and I look up at her quickly. "It's her birthday," she says. "I brought her here for dinner." He looks at me and then over and her.

He gives us a slight smile. "I'll have that right out," he says and walks away. I pull my hand away and she looks at me.

"What the hell was that?" I asked her.

"What do you mean?" she replies, not looking up from her menu. "Really? You're going to play dumb?" I say and laugh.

She looks up at me. "You're too pretty for him," she says.

"You can do better. Anyway, what are you going to order?" she asks, changing the subject. I stay quiet and she looks up at me. I smile and shake my head. The bartender brings out our wine and a different waiter comes out to take our order.

"I think you scared him away," I say teasingly and take a sip of my drink.

"Good. If he liked you, he would have tried harder," she says snapping. We both laugh and continue to talk as we wait for our food. "That was so good," she says as we make our way back to the car.

"I told you, you would like it," I say. "Let's grab more wine and go back to the house."

"You don't want to go out or anything?" she asks.

"We're going out tomorrow," I say.

"All I want to do right now is go home and get out of this dress," I pause.

"And maybe get you out of yours too." She blushes and hits the gas.

It was a little after eleven when I woke up the next morning. Avery is still sleeping so I get out of bed quietly and try not to wake her. I go to the kitchen to grab a glass of water. *I may have had too much wine last night. Last night,* the thought lingered in my head. *I need to stop overthinking this, especially because she's going to be here for two more days.* I take a longer shower than usual. *Trying to wash the guilt away?* I laugh to myself. I can hear Avery talking when I make my way back to the room. I stand in the doorway and watch her for a minute. "We went to that little Italian place you told me about," I hear her say. *Oh, she must be talking to Ivan.*

"It was just us yesterday. One of her friends is throwing her a party tonight. Alex, I think. Yeah… okay babe. I'll see you tomorrow. Love you too, bye." I try to act like I wasn't listening and walk over to my dresses.

"Was that Ivan?" I asked and turned to look at her. *Oh my gosh, she hasn't put her clothes on yet.*

"Yeah. He was calling to see how everything was going. He apologized again for not being able to make it." I smile. It did feel weird not having him around, but that's life. It was going to happen sooner or later. I threw her shirt at her.

"Get up. I'm hungry," I say and head to the kitchen. I hear the shower turn on and I grab my phone to see if I have any messages. I bypass all the happy birthdays, as I do every year, and open a message from Alex. The message had the address for the party and the time he wanted me there.

It also included "I can't wait to see you tonight" at the end. Alex and I were over before we even started, thanks to HER. Part of me has always kind of wondered where it would have gone, but with HER around, I guess we'll never know. I must have been standing there, deep in thought, because I never noticed Avery walk into the kitchen.

"Chloe, hello?" she says, waving her hand.

"What?" I say, still trying to snap out of it.

"What's going on?" she asks with a concerned look on her face. "Nothing, sorry." I laugh. I put my phone down and walked over to the table.

"Do you want me to cook, or should we just go eat somewhere?" I ask.

"Chloe, come one," she says.

"What's going on?" "I was just thinking about tonight," I say.

"Do you not want to go? Or...," she pauses.

"Do you not want to go with me?" I look at her and laugh. She stands there with the same look on her face.

"It's not you. I promise." I say. "Now can we go eat?"

We go to this small restaurant for brunch. It's a nice day out, so we grab a table outside and order some food. I chose this place mainly for their mimosas.

"Starting early, I see," Avery says as she takes a sip of her water. "It's my birthday weekend," I say.

"Here, have one." She's quiet while we eat, and I decide to wait till we're back in the car to say anything. On the way home I take a detour and head towards the park. We pulled up and I turned off the car. "Come on," I say.

"Let's go for a walk." I grabbed a small blanket out of the trunk, and we headed up the hill. We sat in silence for a while, and I looked over at her. She's leaning back with her eyes shut, letting the sun hit her. "I'm glad you're here," I say. She looks over at me, one eye open, and sits up.

"Are you?" she asks.

"You've been in your head all morning."

"I know, I'm sorry," I say.

"I just don't want things to get weird between us." She laughs. "Here we go again," she says. I stay quiet. *I should just tell her.* "You can talk to me. You know that right? Just help me understand," she says. I take a deep breath and proceed to tell everything that happened between me and HER.

"I don't want that to happen to us. You've become so important to me," I say. She doesn't say anything for a minute. I can tell she's trying to process everything I just said, and I let her.

"Come on," I say and stand up. "Let's go back to the house." I'm in the room getting my outfit ready for the night when she walks in.

She walks over to the bed and sits down. "That's not going to happen to us," she says.

"I'm glad you told me." She walks over to me and holds out her pinky. I laugh and hook mine with hers.

"Now let's get dressed," she says excitedly. "We have a party to get to."

It's a little after nine when we arrive. I pulled down the visor to check my makeup one last time in the mirror and sent Alex a text to let him know that I was here. Avery places her hand on my arm.

"You look great Chloe," she says. I put the visor back up and take a deep breath.

"Are you ready for this?" I ask and she nods.

"Happy Birthday!" Everyone yells as we walk in. I'm instantly filled with excitement and anxiety all at once. Alex runs up to me, picks me up and spins me around. *God, I missed him.*

"Put me down, I'm in a dress," I say as I'm laughing. He puts me down and places both hands on my shoulders as he looks me up and down.

"Wow," he says and hugs me again.

"Happy Birthday, Chloe," he whispers in my ear.

"Oh, Alex, this is my friend Avery," I say, and he reaches out his hand.

"Nice to meet you," he says and gives her a kind smile.

"Let me show you to your table and grab you a drink," he says and hooks his arm in mine. I reach back for Avery's hand, but she doesn't meet mine. We make our way to a table in the back and grab our seats. Alex walks away to get our drinks and I turn to look at Avery. "Do you know all of these people?" she asks.

"No," I say. "Alex knows how much I hate a big crowd though, that's why he sat us back here." A few people came up to greet us and to wish me a happy birthday. I introduce Avery to the people I actually know and see her start to relax a little. A few of the girls arrive a little later and sit with us at the table. I introduce them all to Avery and make sure to include her in conversation, so she doesn't feel left out. Alex walks over to us and says hi to everyone.

"Can I steal her for a dance?" he asks Avery.

"Of course, she's all yours." Avery says and we head to the dance floor.

"She's pretty," he says as we're dancing.

"Don't start," I say and roll my eyes.

"Is she the reason you haven't been coming around?" he asks, and I shoot him a "back off" look.

"It's not like that," I say.

"I see the way she looks at you," he says.

"What do you mean?" I ask.

"Well right now she's looking at me like if I move my hand any lower on your back, she'll kill me," he says and laughs. He spins me around and I look over at her. When she notices I'm looking at her she turns and starts talking to the girls.

"She looks at you the way I do," he says. I tilt my head up to look at him, and the music stops.

He smiles. "Go back to the table. I'm going to grab everyone a drink." I walk back to the table and sit down.

Everyone was staring at me. "What?" I ask and look over at Avery.

"Girl, we saw the way Alex was looking at you," one of the girls says from across the table.

"Please, Alex looks at every girl like that," I say, and we all laugh.

"No, everyone looks at you like that," I hear and look up to meet HER gaze. She was standing at the edge of the table, staring at me with that insolent smile.

"Happy Birthday, Chloe," she says, and my heart begins to race. *Why the hell is she here?*

"And who's this?" she asks, looking at Avery.

"I don't think we've had the pleasure of meeting. I'm…" "Leaving," I say as I stand and cut her off. Alex was walking back towards the table with a tray of shots. He looked over at HER and set the tray down.

"Well, you heard her. You should go," he says and turns his attention backlit he table. She laughed and shook her head. We watched as she began to walk away, and she stopped and turned around.

"I'd be careful if I were you," she says as she looks at Avery and turns to continue to walk away. Avery stared at her with a confused look on her face and turned her attention towards me.

"Now, who wants shots?" Alex yells out, breaking the awkwardness. We all laugh as he passes them around and then raise our glasses.

"To the birthday girl," he says, and everyone cheers.

"I have to pee," I say and look at Avery, who's suddenly glued to her phone.

"Come with me?" I asked her and we headed to the bathroom. "He seems nice," she says.

"Oh no, not you too," I say back to her, and we laugh.

"I'm serious though. The two of you would look good together," she says as I wash my hands.

"Yeah," I say, trying to end the conversation. "So, was that…" she starts to ask.

"We should get back," I say before she can finish.

"Thanks for the party, Alex. We're heading out already," I say. He had spent the last half hour at ta separate table with Her and couple of the girls. He gave me a half smile and a side hug before I left. He must of been pretty drunk because that was not like him, but I don't overthink it. We get back to the house and I head straight to the room and change. I hear my phone go off as I climb into bed. It was a text from one of the girls. Attached were pictures from the party, and I went through them as I laid back. I'm smiling at my phone when Avery walks in the room.

"I got pics from the party," I say holding my phone up. Come look at them with me," I say and pat the bed, signaling her to come lay down. We go through the pics and laugh. There's pics of us walking in when they all yelled "Happy birthday" and a bunch of me and all the girls. I continue to scroll through them, and a picture of Avery and I pops up.

"Aw," she says. "You always look so serious." I scowl at her, and we both laugh. The last picture is of me and Alex, from our dance. My arms are wrapped sound his neck and his are wrapped around my waist. We're just staring at each other, smiling. I stared at it a little too long and Avery turned to look at me.

"Was it just me or did Alex's attitude change as we were leaving the party?" I ask.

"I'm not sure. I don't know him like you do," she says. She looks at the picture again and I can tell she wants to ask me something.

"That was HER right? The girl at the party," she asks. I never wanted Avery to know that part of my life. It was drama, it was messy, and I didn't want her getting caught up in it. I also didn't want to lie to her and ruin what we had. So any questions she had, I would answer.

"Yes. That was her," I say. She nods and looked down at her hands. "What about you and Alex. What the story there?" She asks. *I better sit up for this.*

"We used to talk," I say.

"Alex and I."

"What happened?" she asks. I don't say anything for a minute. "We don't have to..." I put my hand up to stop her.

"Remember when I told you about HER?" She nods.

"We were drinking one night. Alex and I had already gone out a few times and I had already stopped things with her. She was there that night. Alex and I were standing on the back porch talking and she had been watching the whole time. I leaned in to kiss him and she just…blew up." Avery was quiet.

"It got messy so before it got any worse, I left. I stopped going around and that's it. It was over before it even began," I say.

"So, wait, I'm confused. You ended it just like that?" she asks. I nod. "Just like that," I say.

"Why not talk to him about it though? I mean, if you liked him, why did you just walk away?" she asked.

"Because they're friends," I say.

"I don't believe in making people choose."

"What do you mean?" she asks and sits up.

"When you're with someone, all you see is them. If they're important to you, then there is nobody else, it's just them," I say.

"And if there is somebody else, then that one person isn't as important to you as you thought they were to begin with. That's why I'll never make anyone choose. If there's somebody else, then the answer is clear if you ask me." She doesn't say anything.

"Can we go to bed now?" I ask. "I'm exhausted."

I woke up the next morning and Avery was not in bed. I headed into the bathroom to wash up and then went into the kitchen to find her. Nothing. I walked back into the bedroom and noticed that all her things are gone. *She left*. I looked for my phone to see if I had any messages from her, but there was none, not even a call. I go to type out a message, but end up just staring at my phone, trying to replay the events of last night. *Did I say something to upset her? My head was pounding. I'm too hungover for this*. I grab some clothes to take a shower and go back to bed after. I wake up to the sound of my phone ringing and roll over to grab it.

"Hey Alex," I say sleepily.

"Wow, you're still in bed?" he says laughing. "You're becoming a light weight."

"Shut up," I say laughing. "I was thinking we could have dinner," he says.

"Oh gosh, I'm still in bed. I don't feel like getting dressed," I say.

"Not a problem. I can come to you," he says. *He's not going to take no for an answer*.

"Okay, that works," I say.

"Great. I'll pick up some food. See you in a bit," he says and hangs up. I lay in bed for a few more minutes before I decided to get up. I heard a knock at the door while I was in the bathroom throwing my hair up. Alex was standing there with food and a bottle of wine. *I can't even think about alcohol right now.*

"I was going to grab us tacos, but I grabbed us food from the little Italian place you like instead," he says as he walks into the kitchen. We sit at the table and talk a little about the party last night while we eat our food. He clears the table for us and grabs two glasses for the wine.

"Your friend seemed nice," he says. *There it is. I'm surprised it took him this long to say anything.*

"Yeah, she's cool. Don't even think about it. She's taken," I say, giving him a serious look. He raises his eyebrows.

"She has to be, if she's talking to you right?" he asks teasingly. I smacked his arm.

"It's not like that. I already told you," I say laughing.

"We're just friends." He smiles at me.

"Okay, I believe you," he says and takes a sip of his wine.

"I've missed you," he says.

"Me too," I say.

"Sorry for storming out the other night," I say.

"I wanted to leave before it escalated. You know I hate drama." He nods his head.

"I know. I just wish you wouldn't have shut me out the way you did." I let out a deep breath.

"I just didn't know how to go about it," I say.

"You were friends before I ever came into the picture. I had my thing with HER and then started with you and just made a mess of things." We're both quiet for a minute.

"I just think everything's still so fresh right now and it's better to let things cool down before we think of trying again. I don't want to get in between your friendship," I say. He smiles.

"So, you're saying I still have a chance?" and we laugh.

A few days go by and still no word from Avery, and I chose not to reach out either. Alex and I kept in touch, and he called one night to invite me out for drinks with him and the girls.

As I was getting ready, I heard my phone ring and go to pick it up thinking it was Alex. 'Hello," I say.

"What's up?" I hear on the other end of the phone.

"You know what this weekend is right?" It was Ivan. I stay quiet, trying to process him being on the phone.

"Okay, I'll tell you," he says. "It's the first weekend of football!" he says excitedly. *How is it already football season?*

"How could I forget?" I say.

"Okay, so pack your stuff and come stay with us for the weekend," he says.

"We can't miss a game, Chloe. We never do."

"I know," I say.

"I have plans tonight though. I promise I'll be there in the morning." He lets out a deep breath.

"Okay. Don't drink too much. Have fun and we'll see you tomorrow." *Where did the time go? I never forget the football season. It's my favorite time of the year.* I brush it off and continue getting ready. I pull up to Alex's house and he meets me at the door. He gives me a hug and a kiss on the cheek, and we head inside. The girls are looking at me when I walk in with a look, I'm not really sure of. They quickly say hi and Alex hands me a drink.

"Are we staying in or going out?" one of the girls asks.

"We should go out," Cee says and everyone else agrees.

"Let's finish our drinks and then we can leave," Alex says.

"How long has that been going on?" Cee asks as we walk out to our cars. I try to play dumb like I don't know what she's talking about. "What do you mean?" I ask.

"Oh, please. We all saw the two of you on the porch," she says. "Nothing's going on," I say and get in my car before she can say anything else. The last thing I needed was for any of the girls to start talking about this, or HER to find out. We got to the bar and once we settled in, I pulled Alex to the side.

"Look, I know you mean anything by it, but can we keep the PDA to a minimum?" I say. He looked at me confused and then laughed. "The PDA?" he asks and laughs again. I roll my eyes.

"The girls saw us on the porch," I say.

"So?" he asks.

"I greet all of you like that. We'll besides the kissing," he says with a smile.

"I know. I just don't want us to be the topic of discussion anytime they're around each other. This isn't the first time they've questioned it either," I say.

"So let them question it. I don't want to hide you, Chloe. You're who I want to be with, and if they don't want to see it, then they don't have to come around," he says. I smile at him. He's right. I don't care who finds out and who doesn't. I just want to enjoy my night.

We drink, we laugh, and I finally relax. I see Cee look down at her phone, turn over and look at me then towards the door. It was HER, of course it was. I look around for Alex so I can let him know I'm leaving, but she's already at the table. She says hi to everyone and takes a seat. Alex comes up to us and I stand and grab my things. He doesn't say hi to her, he just stares at me.

"Wow Alex, you're not even going to say hi?" she asks. He says nothing and doesn't take his eyes off me. He has a worried look on his face. I turn and face the girls, wishing them all a good night.

"I'll leave with you," Alex says.

"No, it's fine. You should stay. We'll talk soon," I say.

Just as I turn to leave, I hear HER say from across the table "Are you going to tell her, or should I?" I look at her and then at him and suddenly the whole room is quiet.

"Tell me what?" I ask and turn to face Alex. No one says anything and I just shake my head.

"I don't have time for this," I say.

"We slept together," she says. "The night of your birthday party when you were with that girl.

"I turn to look at Alex, trying to hold back the rage that had overcome me.

"It hurts, doesn't it?" She asks. I stormed out of the bar, I could hear Alex not too far behind me.

"Chloe!" I hear him yell out.

"Chloe, wait!" I tried to get in my car as quick as I could, but before I knew it, he was standing in between me and the door.

"Alex, move," I say as sternly as possible. I could hear the shakiness in my voice.

"She got in my head Chloe," he says, still trying to catch his breath. I laugh. He can't be serious.

"That's your excuse?" I ask.

"Just hear me out. When she showed up at your party that night, I was just as shocked as you were. I went up to their table to have a drink and she was just going on and on about your friend being there. She kept talking about how you put your own feelings before one else's. That you don't care about how the person you're sleeping with feels, as long as you're getting what you want out of it. And once you become bored, you throw them away. She said that's what you were doing with me, and it was happening right in front of my face. Just like it happened with her." He stared at me, eyes begging for forgiveness as he waited for me to respond. I open my car door and watch as he takes a step towards me.

"Well, at least now the two of you can be miserable together," I say and get in my car and leave. I drive home in silence. My phone keeps going off, but I don't bother to look at it. When I get home, I go straight to the fridge and grab a beer. *I shouldn't be surprised. I mean, it's HER. She's doing it to get back at me, and she did a good job of reeling him right in.* I finish my beer and get ready for bed. I want nothing more than for this night to be over.

I lay in bed for a while when I woke up the next morning. I look for my phone, dreading to see the missed calls and texts that await me.

I hear it ringing in the kitchen. *Ugh, it's too early for this. Shit, it's Ivan.* "Hi," I say, trying to sound cheerful and awake.

"Hey! What time are you planning on taking off?" he asks. *I haven't even packed yet.*

"I'm almost done packing. I just need to change, so maybe in an hour," I say.

"Perfect! I'm going to the store to get some stuff so I can cook. I can't wait for you to see our house," he says. I can tell how excited he is, and I feel bad because I'm not in the mood.

"Can't wait," I say, and we hang up. I take a quick shower and pack as quickly as I can. I have a few minutes to spare and go through my messages. There are messages from Alex and Cee. *Why was she messaging me?* After reading a few, I realized they were from HER.

"Believe it or not, it wasn't that hard to convince Alex you were with that girl, or that you were a horrible person. Who is she anyway? Your next victim? It'd be a shame if she found out who you really are. She seems so innocent. Do you really want her to end up like me and Alex?" She's obviously still pissed about the whole situation, but Alex on the other hand was the complete opposite.

"Please talk to me. Can I come over? I was drunk, I don't even remember." I send Ivan a message to let him know I'm on the way and get on the road. Maybe I can talk to him about everything after the game. At Least he'll be happy that I'm not hungover. I started thinking about Avery. I still haven't talked to her since she left that weekend. I hope it's not weird, I would really like to just enjoy my day.

I pull up to Ivans' about an hour later. He practically runs out of the front door and almost tackles me. I missed him.

"Avery's in the shower," he says and gives me a tour of the house. It's cute, and even though I've only been here for five minutes, it feels like home. He grabs two beers and leads me to the guest bedroom.

"You can put your things in here. I'm going to start the grill," he says. I put my bag down on the bed and pulled out my phone. I block Alex and Cee's numbers. I don't want either of them trying to get a hold of me today. I walk out of the room right as Avery's coming out of the bathroom.

"Hey," I say, and she freezes. She looks like she's just seen a ghost.

"What are you…" she pauses, trying to find the words to say.

"Where's Ivan?" she asks, finally.

"He went out back to start the grill," I say.

"Right. Okay," she says, still looking at me very shocked. She walks past me and heads out back. *Did she not know I was coming? Surely Ivan let her know*. I wait for a moment before I go outside. I wanted to give them time to discuss my arrival in case there was a fight. When I finally walk outside, they're talking about what he wanted her to make.

"What do you think we should have?" Ivan turns and asks me. "Something simple," I say.

"I can help with whatever you decide," I turn to Avery. She smiles, nods her head and walks back inside. I sat down at the table with Ivan.

"So, did you get drunk last night?" he asks smiling. I laugh.

"Not even a little," I say. He looks at me confused.

"I thought you went out last night?" he asks.

"Oh, I did," I say and start thinking about everything that happened. "It..." I pause and shake my head.

"What happened?" he asks, sitting up straight in his chair. I take a deep breath.

"Can we talk about it later? I really want to have a good day." I say.

"Okay. We'll talk later," he says and rests his hand on mine. I smile and nod my head.

"I'm going to see if Avery needs any help," I say.

"Okay, I need to get this food started before the game starts," he says, and I get up and walk inside. Avery was standing in the kitchen, lost in thought when I walked in. I set my beer on the counter and asked if I could help with anything.

She doesn't speak. "Hello, Avery?" I say, waving my hand in front of her face.

"What? Sorry," she says and turns away.

"I asked if you needed help with anything," I said. She stares at me. "I didn't know... I mean, you're here," she says.

"Yeah," I say and laugh. She grabs the bridge of her nose.

"I'm sorry. I'm being super weird right now," she laughs and grabs a drink out of the fridge.

"Are you okay?" I ask.

"Yes. I'm… I'm good," she says. We start getting the sides ready and taking things out to Ivan.

"You didn't know I was coming, did you?" I ask.

"No. I mean, yes. I knew you were coming. I've just been in my head a lot lately," she says. I reach out and grab her shoulder and she freezes.

"Calm down," I say, and she relaxes.

"Do you want to talk about it?" I ask,

"I do. Can we wait till later?" she asks. I nod my head in agreement, and we finish in the kitchen and join Ivan outside.

He finishes the food just as the game was about to start and we hurried inside. Ivan has always been a good cook. Hell, he can cook better than I can. I look over at him and nod to let him know the food was excellent, as I always do, and he smiles. It was an exciting first half and during the break Avery gets up to take our plates to the kitchen. I offered to help, but she just asked me to grab us all another round. I get back from the kitchen, set Avery's drink down on the table and hand Ivan another beer. I sit back and he sighs.

"What's up?" I asked, looking over at him. "I think she's starting to miss home. She's been so distant since she came back after your birthday," he says quietly. I stay quiet, giving him time to explain further. *She's been distant with me too.*

"She called me that morning to tell me she was going to see them, and she would see me later that night," he continued. I breathe, finally. *Maybe it has nothing to do with me after all.*

"Maybe I'm just overthinking," he says. I placed my hand on his arm.

"Everything is going to be fine," I say and give him a reassuring smile. We watched the rest of the game and when we won Avery and I laughed at Ivan as he jumped around the living room. He settles down after about fifteen minutes and we all relax.

"So," he says, trying to slow his breathing.

"Tell me about last night." I let out a deep breath. *I was hoping he would forget.*

"Oh, I can go to the room," Avery says. Ivan looks at her and then over at me, as if asking me if she needs to leave.

"No, you don't have to," I say, and she sits back down. I start telling them about Alex, which Avery has already heard, but she listens anyway. I told him about how we had reconnected after my birthday and all the time we had been spending together. Ivan seems surprised, especially because I tell him everything and have never mentioned Alex to him. Avery, on the other hand, looks like she can't wait for this conversation to be over. Then I got to what happened last night.

"And apparently they slept together," I say.

"I've always hated HER. I was so glad when you finally decided to end things," Ivan said.

"You know HER?" Avery says, looking almost as surprised that she said that she said that as we were to hear it.

"I should be asking you the same thing," he says and laughs. He turns his attention back towards me.

"So, have you heard from either of them?" he asks. "Of course. They blew my phone up all night," I say. I handed my phone to him, and together, they read the message.

"First of all, being drunk is never an excuse" Avery says.

"Please tell me that you've blocked him," he says.

"Don't worry. I did that this morning," I say.

"Good, he doesn't deserve you," he says.

"Anyway. It happened, and it's over," I say.

"Thanks for today, I really needed it." They both look at me and smile. "Now, if you don't mind, I think I'd like to shower and lay down. I think I'm starting to feel the alcohol." We all laugh, and I make my way to the room to grab my things.

I sit in bed for a while after my shower. It felt good to be away and not be alone. I guess I'm not all that upset about Ivan's move after all. It gives me somewhere to escape to when I need it. My phone buzzes next to me. *Who could possibly be messaging me this late*? It was Avery. "Are you awake?" I read. I was so focused on telling Ivan about everything that happened last night, that I forgot Avery wanted to talk.

"Yes. Come in, the door is open," I reply. A few minutes after I heard a light knock at the door, and she walked in.

"I saw the light on. You weren't getting ready for bed, were you?" she asks.

"No, it's fine. I'm sorry I forgot you wanted to talk," I say.

"Don't apologize, you had a lot on your mind," she says. I look at her confused.

"With everything that happened..." she says, starting to look confused herself.

"Oh, yeah," I say, waiving it off.

"Enough about me. Tell me about you. Is everything okay?" I ask. She looks at me for a second but doesn't say anything.

"Does it have anything to do with the fact that you left without saying bye on my birthday?" She gets up from the bed.

"I'm going to need a drink for this. Do you want one? I'll just bring you one," she says and walks out of the room. She walks back in with a bottle of vodka, a mixer and two glasses that were already made. She hands me a drink and leans on the dresses. I watched her, waiting for her to start. She moves over to a seat by the nightstand.

"Whenever you're ready," I say laughing. She gets up again and sits on the edge of the bed.

"You said something that night," she starts. *Fuck.*

"It just really made me think about a lot of stuff. I didn't even sleep that night. I just laid there next to you. I got up early, grabbed my things and went to my mom's," she says. "Why didn't you wake me up?" I ask.

"The same reason you didn't call when you realized I was gone," she says.

I nod my head. "What did I say?" I ask, not really wanting to know the answer.

"You don't remember?" she asks. I shake my head shamefully. "Wow, I didn't think you were that drunk," she says, and I laugh.

"Me either," I say.

"You were saying that when you loved someone, you only saw them. And if you ever find yourself looking at someone else, then maybe you don't love your person the way you think you do," she says. I stay quiet and then turn to look at her.

"Well, I don't think I said those exact words," I say and take a sip of my drink.

"I like your version better if I'm being honest." We both laugh. "Wait, I'm trying to be serious," she says, trying to hold in her laugh. "It just made me think. I love Ivan. Does sneaking around with you make me love him less?" Her question stuns me.

"I don't think so. It sounds wrong, but it's just sex. We don't have feelings for each other. We've already talked about this," I say. She stares down at her drink.

"We don't have to do this. If you think that hooking up will jeopardize your relationship in any way, then we can stop. I promise it won't affect our friendship," I say.

"Well, I didn't say all that," she says, and I laugh. "I just said it made me think."

"Yeah, think so much that you ran out on me and have been avoiding me," I say teasingly.

She scrunches her face. "I'm sorry." I smile.

"Don't worry about it. I'm glad we can talk about these things. Just tell me next time instead of running out on me. It hurts my ego a bit," I say and nudge her shoulder.

"Deal," she says. "Also, maybe you should give Ivan some reassurance," she looks at me confused.

"He mentioned you've been distance lately and thinks you're missing home," I say.

"Shit," she says and puts her hand on her head. "I didn't think it was noticeable."

"I told him not to overthink it. The two of you will be just fine," I say.

"Let's finish these and go to bed." She gives me a tight hug and leaves the room.

I woke up the next morning to the sound of music and the smell of breakfast. I put some clothes on and walked into the kitchen. Avery's dancing around cooking and I take a seat at the table and watch her. She doesn't hear me come in and when she turns around, I burst into laughter. "You're in a good mood this morning," I say as I get up and grab a glass of water.

"I didn't realize how much I needed to have that talk," she says. I smile.

"I'm going to go wash up," I say.

"Okay, the food is almost done," she says. We sit down to eat and talk a little about everything that's been going on since the last time we talked.

"I'm sorry for everything that happened with Alex the other night. That was pretty shitty of them both," she says. I wanted to show Avery the messages from HER, even though I knew it would lead to questions. I took a deep breath and pulled up the messages and handed her the phone. I watch her facial expression change as she begins to read the messages and instantly regret it. *I think I'm going to be sick.* She sets the phone down when she's done and uses the food around on her place.

"Avery?" I said nervously. My heart was racing, and I felt my throat begin to tighten. *What's happening?*

"I feel like you didn't tell me everything about HER up on the hill that day," she says. There was a lot that I left out, purposely. Avery was supposed to be a onetime thing, not whatever this is. Definitely not a friend. The sick feeling in my stomach was not going away, in fact, it was getting worse. "Chloe," she says.

"I didn't tell you everything," I say. I could hear the tremble in my voice.

"I don't date women." I watch as her head tilted slightly as she processed what I had just said.

"But you..." Avery said, as she paused and sat up in her seat. "I don't. I never have. I just...sleep with them," I say.

"You just sleep with them?" She asked. *I should of kept the messages to myself.*

"Yes, Avery. I just sleep with them. I've never had a relationship with a woman before. I never wanted the emotional connection. I like the sex. And that's all it was with HER," I say as she cuts me off.

"How long?" She asked. Her voice was more high pitched this time. I'm assuming because this was her first time hearing about it.

"It went on for two years," I say. She jumped out of her seat. "Two years Chloe? And you're upset because she acted a certain way towards you? I'm not sticking up for her, more making excuses for her actions, but you can't do that to people." I was completely taken aback by her reaction.

And more than anything, I felt judged. "It's not like she didn't know," I exclaim as I remove myself from my seat. Again, I watched as the puzzled look returned to her face.

"Any woman I've hooked up with knew I was strictly sex for me. I was always sure to let it be known so there wouldn't be any confusion. She was no different. I reminded her time and time again that it was just sex."

I took a deep breath as I waited for her to respond. "Why have we never had that conversation?" Her voice became flat as if she was trying to hide emotion.

"What?" I ask. My body had become full of adrenaline, and I was trying to steady my breathing.

"This is the first time I'm hearing about the "only sex" thing. You haven't sat me down for that conversation," she says. *How could I not have had this discussion with her*? I take a seat at the table and look over at Avery. She follows my lead and sits next to me as she wats for an answer.

"Uhm, I don't know why I never told you. It's usually one of the first things I do. I guess it was just because of …" "Ivan," we both say. "Yeah," I say and chuckle. "I guess I figured since we've had the conversation about having feelings for each other that you'd pick up on the no dating thing."

My hands became sweaty as I waited for some kind of response. The sound of her laugh catches me off guard.

"Sorry. I was trying to relate in some kind of way, but if I'm being honest, we're the complete opposite." I sit up in my seat, waiting for her to explain. She sits back and I was confused at how relaxed she had become.

"I've only every dated women. In fact, Ivan is the first guy I've ever been with," she says. I could practically feel my jaw hit the floor. "It is very different. I will admit to that, but dating women isn't' as. Bad as you make it seem. I think you're just afraid to feel love on a deeper lever than what you're used too." *I hate the way she reads me, but the more it happens, the more drawn I become.* I could feel myself begin to smile and laughed when she started to shake her head.

"You are so unserious, Chloe. It's irritating," she says as she rolls her eyes.

"So, are you going to talk to Alex about it?" she asks.

"I thought I'd just avoid it," I say smiling. She gives me a concerned look.

"I mean, what's the point? He's just going to apologize, say he was drunk and that it will never happen again," I say.

"At least you'll get some kind of an apology though," she says. "I like my idea better," I say, and she rolls her eyes. I stayed there for a few more hours and then I headed back home. I think about calling Alex on the drive back, but I don't do it. I think I'll wait a few more days.

I turn onto my street and from a distance I can see a vehicle in my driveway. As I got closer, I realized who it was. *You've got to be kidding me.* She looks like she hasn't slept in days.

"What are you doing here?" I ask as I get out of the car, not looking at HER at all. I get my bag out of the trunk and walk up the porch steps past her as she stands there looking lost.

"Can we talk, please?" she asks.

"I have nothing to say to you," I say and walk through the door. "You don't have to talk, I just need you to listen," she says, and she follows me inside.

"So, talk," I say, already hearing the frustration in my voice. "I'm sorry," she says, and I roll my eyes.

"I loved you. I still love you. I know I'm not supposed to, and I know we talked about this when we first started, but I can't help it. I didn't know what to do when you told me we had to stop. I didn't know how to leave you alone. So, I kept showing up to Alex's, hoping I'd at least be able to see you. I wanted to talk to you on your birthday to tell you I'd put my feelings aside and if we could still be friends, but then I saw you, with another girl. My heart dropped, but that hurt instantly turned into bitterness. I kept thinking, *how the hell did she move on so fast*, but I mean look at you. Anyone would be lucky to get even an ounce of your attention. You know what really caught my attention over everything else? The fact that you had her out in public, at your birthday party. She obviously means more to you than I did in the two years you were sleeping with me. So, between seeing you with her, and knowing you've been hanging out with Alex, I knew I had lost you for good. Sleeping with him was stupid and I have no excuse for it, other than just wanting to hurt you. So, I'm sorry." Tears were rolling down her face and I stayed quiet. I had no words, just this unexplainable feeling in my chest.

"You should go," I say quietly. She stares at me in disbelief, and I walk over to the door. She turns slowly, takes one last look at me and leaves. I feel like I should be pissed, but I'm not. I'm upset. I hurt HER. I laid in bed and stared at the ceiling as my mind began to race. *I had no idea I made her feel that way.* I thought that by explaining what I wanted from the beginning that I would save her from this. You can't just sleep with someone and spend time with them and expect them not to develop feelings at some point. I'm going to have to talk to her and apologize. I don't want my apology to be confused with me wanting to start again though. *Did anyone else feel like this? How many people have I hurt?*

A few days passed and all I can think about is the mess that I had made. *I do not want to do that anymore, to anyone. Should I tell Avery?* We've had too many conversations about this already, and we haven't done anything recently. We should be good. During lunch I got a call from one of the girls.

"Hey Lex," I say, answering the phone. Lex and I had become close over the past several years. She didn't care much for the drama, and never put herself in the middle of anything that was going on. I liked that about her.

"Let's grab lunch," she says.

"I want a mimosa."

"I'll meet you in fifteen?" I ask.

"Yes! I'm excited," she says, and I laugh. I could use the distraction. I clock out of work and head over to the restaurant. She's already sitting at a table outside when I pull up. There's another girl with her who I didn't recognize. *Maybe they work together.*

"Chloe!" she yells out as I turn the corner and make my way to the table. She runs up to hug me, squeezing me tight, and I hug her back.

"Hi Lex," I say laughing. I loved her energy. She was always so happy anytime you saw her, and it just made everyone want to be around her. "Chloe, this is Sara," she says, and I reach my hand out.

"It's nice to meet you," I say and smile. I sit down just as the waitress bring us our drink.

"Are we just drinking, or should we order food too?" I ask and the girls laugh. We talked and ordered some appetizers. I told her about the conversation I had with HER after the incident at the party.

"I think you need a little get away," she says and looks over at Sara.

"We're taking a girls trip in a few weeks," she says.

"We were thinking about getting a cabin. Sitting around, drinking some wine. Just a relaxing weekend," Sara says.

"We can go out one night too," Lex says, and I laugh.]

"You can bring whoever you want." I think about it for a few minutes.

"You know what, I'm in," I say and we all cheer.

"I'm so happy you're coming," Lex says and gives me a hug. "Thanks for today. It was fun. Oh, and it was nice to meet you Sara," I say and give her a smile. Lex looks over at me and waves before she gets in her car and leaves. I know I shouldn't be, but I'm still thinking about HER. Hurting her was never my intention. I keep thinking about the look on her face that night. My phone rings, bringing me out of my thoughts, it was Avery.

"Hi Avery," I say, answering the phone.

"Hey," I hear her say followed by

"Hey! What's up" coming from Ivan. I was clearly on speaker phone. "Do you have anything planned this weekend?" he asks.

"I thought we were watching the game?" I ask, slightly confused.

"I have to work," he says. I can tell that he's annoyed.

"You can still come over though," he says.

"Your new job sucks," I say, and he laughs.

"The money doesn't though," he says.

"You could have just called her on your phone," Avery says, annoyed and I can't help but to laugh again. "Aww Avery," I say.

"Don't be jealous babe," Ivan says.

"Oh, shut up. Both of you," Avery says.

"Why don't you just come stay over here Avery?" I ask.

"You know, so you don't feel left out." Ivan was still laughing, and I heard what sounded like a smack.

"You know what, I think that's a great idea. So much of a great idea that I think I'll pack and leave tomorrow after work," she says. "Wait, tomorrow?" Ivan says and now Avery's the one that's laughing. "Okay. Well, I guess I will see you on whatever day you choose to come," I say laughing.

"You two have a great night."

I got home from work the next day and realized I needed a few things from the grocery store. I got a text from Avery on the way there, letting me know she's on her way. *I thought she was kidding about coming a day early. I guess I'll grab stuff for dinner. I think I'll make tacos. That's easy enough.* I'm standing in the meat aisle when I hear a voice that makes me freeze immediately.

"Tacos huh?" I hear. I turned around and saw Alex. He's standing with his hands in his pockets but doesn't look at me. I turn back around, grab what I need and walk away.

"Can you just wait a second?" he asks. I turn around so he won't scream out loud again and cause a scene.

"Stop following me. I have nothing to say to you and I don't want to hear anything you have to say to me," I say.

"Oh, but you can talk to HER?" he asks.

"What we talked about is none of your business," I snapped at him.

"I hurt her, and you hurt me. Now drop it. I have to go." He says nothing and I walk away.

I never walked out of a store so fast, I'm practically out of breath when I get to my car. *I need a drink.* I unload the groceries and head into my room to change into something more comfortable. *Did she tell him that we talked, or that she talked? How else would he know?* Avery walks through the front door, disrupting my thoughts.

"Mm, it smells good in here," she says and walks over to see what I'm making.

"Ooh, tacos. I'll cut up some limes. I brought wine too," she says. She goes to the room to put her things down and proceeds to cut up the limes. She walks over to me and turns my face towards hers. "You're upset. Why are you upset?" she asks, still holding my face. I place my hands on hers and pull them down.

"I'm not," I say and give her a convincing smile.

"I was letting you get all your energy out. Now unhand me and go set the table," I say.

"You're a bad liar," she says and grabs the plates. We sat down to eat, and I poured us each a glass of wine.

"I thought you were joking about coming early," I say, as I watch her take a picture of her food." I was, but I thought why not take a long weekend. I'm sending this to Ivan by the way, to let him know I made it," she says. We continue to eat our food and she tells me all about her work week as I try to pay attention. I do not want the thought of either of them to ruin another one of my weekends. We finish eating and Avery clears the table.

"Leave the dishes in the sink. I'll wash them tomorrow," I say. She comes back to the table and refills our glasses.

"So, are you going to tell me what's wrong?" she asks. I stand up and grab my glass.

"Let's go sit out back," I say, and she follows me. We sat down on the porch swing, and she looked over at me. I stay quiet trying to figure out where to start, so I just pick the beginning.

"She came over here the night I got back from your house. She was standing on the porch when I pulled up," I say. Avery looked shocked. I told her everything she said. All the words I'll never forget. "I feel so bad. I know I shouldn't, but I do. I never want to make anyone feel that way again," I say. I put my head down and she grabs my and. "You can't blame yourself for that, Chloe. She knew exactly what she was getting herself into. I know it sucks, but you can't keep feeling guilty about it," she says.

"What if it was you?" I ask, without even thinking. The question silences her as she stares out into the night. Avery was a master at hiding her emotions. Her face rarely gave her away. She had this sort of calmness to her that always kept me guessing. Though it was aggravating at times, it was fascinating as well.

"Anyway. On top of all that, I ran into Alex at the store. He was pissed that I talked to her, and wouldn't talk to him," I laughed a little. "I just really want to disappear for a few days," I said. *The trip.*

"What trip?" she asks. *I thought I said that to myself.* "I had lunch with my friend Lex the other day. She invited me on a girl's trip in a few weeks," I say.

"Girl's trip huh?" she says, raising an eyebrow. "That actually sounds fun."

"You should come with me. It probably won't be anything crazy, but we're getting a cabin," I say. She nods her head.

"Okay. I'll tell Ivan when I get back home," she says. We sit outside a little while longer before we go back inside.

"I'm going to take a quick shower," I say, grabbing my clothes. "Is it because of Ivan?" I hear her ask as I'm rinsing the soap out of my hair.

"Avery, what the hell?" I say sliding the shower door open just enough to look at her. "I'm in the shower."

"Obviously. I've seen you naked, stop avoiding the question," she says. I close the shower door and continue bathing.

"Is what because of Ivan?" I ask.

"The reason you're so worried that you'll hurt me. Is it because of your friendship with Ivan?" she asks, and I laugh.

"What's so funny?" she asks and slides the shower door open. I quickly slid it shut.

"Step away from the door," I say, still laughing.

"Go back to the room. I'm almost done." She stomps out of the bathroom. I think about her question while I finish my shower. *What does my friendship with Ivan have to do with it*? I walk into the room and find her sitting on the bed with her arms crossed. She's glaring at me.

"Are you pouting?" I asked and threw my towel at her. "Are you going to answer my question?" she asks. I sat down in front of her, pulling her arms away from her chest.

"What does our friendship have to do with this?" I ask.

"If you hurt me, or we fight and stop talking, then you won't come around anymore. I won't be the only one losing you, he'll lose you too. He'll pay for my selfish needs," she says. *I've never thought about that. I've never had to deal with the fact that if I hurt someone, their partner pays the price too.*

"Then we won't let it get to that," I say, trying to reassure her. "We made a promise, remember. The moment one of us starts feeling something more, we speak about it. If we continue, of course," I say.

"If we continue?" she asks. She lunges forward at me, pinning me to the bed.

"Yes, if," I say laughing and we go to bed.

We spent the next couple of days together laughing and enjoying each other's company. I had never been this close to anyone I was hooking up with. I had never seen the point of it, but it was different with her. She was more than just a hookup, she was my friend. We decided to stay in Saturday night, drinking wine and watching movies. I look over at her and just admire her for a second.

"Thank you for being here," I say, and she turns to face me. "I didn't realize how much I needed this, with everything that's been going on."

"I'm always going to be here," she says. "Promise me something," I say, grabbing her hand.

"Promise me that we'll always be friends first." She puts her glass down and puts both of her hands in mine. "I promise that I'll never let anything come between our friendship. You've become my favorite person, Chloe. I think that's part of the reason why we both question things that happen between us. I sure didn't expect it to be like this after the first night," she says and laughs.

"But I don't regret it."

"Well, that makes two of us," I say and grab our drinks. I woke up in the middle of the night, realizing we had both fallen asleep on the couch. She looks so comfortable. I don't want to wake her up. I find the remote and turn off the T.V. "Avery," I say quietly. She opens her eyes, looking at me sleepily.

"Let's go lay on the bed. It will be more comfortable," I say. She grabs my arm and pulls me back down on the couch.

"I'm comfortable like this," she says, wrapping her arms around me, and we fall back asleep. I'm hot when I get up. We slept body to body last night and I feel sweaty. I roll off the couch slowly, trying not to wake her.

"Good morning," she says as I stand up. "Where are you going?" "I need to shower. We give off too much body heat to be sleeping on the couch," I say. I scrunch my face and she laughs. I go into the room to grab some clothes and check my phone. There was a text from Lex. "Hey! Want to grab brunch tomorrow? I want to show you some of the cabins we've picked out." I read.

"Sounds great. Sorry I'm just seeing your message. Let me know what time you want to meet." I send back. I walk into the bathroom and find Avery already in the shower.

"Good, you're already showering. We're going to have brunch with Lex to talk about the trip," I say. She pops her head out of the shower.

"Okay. Come in so we can leave quicker. I'm starving," she says. I smile and shake my head. "I'm not showering with you. So, hurry," I say. She rolls her eyes and slides the shower door shut. "Do you want me to grab your clothes?" I ask as I start to wash up. I heard the water stop and watched her come out. She grabs a towel and wraps herself.

"I can grab them. Get in, it's your turn," she says. I undress and get in the shower. I hear the door slide open and before I can open my eyes and turn around, I feel her arms around me, and I freeze.

"What are you doing?" I ask, gasping as I try to catch my breath. "Showering. Just relax," she says softly. She pours soap into her hand

and starts to lather it across my body. I stay quiet, trying my best not to look at her. As soon as I'm done, I jump out of the shower, quickly grab a towel and go to the room. She walks in minutes later and I'm still sitting on my bed. She looks at me confused.

"What's wrong," she asks as she walks towards me. I get off the bed and walk over to the dresser.

"You shouldn't have done that," I say and walk back into the bathroom to change.

"Why are you being so weird about it? It's nothing I haven't seen before," she says.

"Just get dressed. I don't want to be late," I say. We drive in silence on the way to meet Lex. When we arrived, I started to get out of the car, and she pulled me back in.

"I'm not walking into the restaurant like this. Tell me what's happening. What did I do?" she asks. *I don't want to walk in like this either*.

"I promise we'll talk when we get back to the house," I say. She holds out her pinky, giving me a serious look. I hook mine in hers and nod.

"Come on. Let's go in." I say. Lex is already sitting at a table when we walk in. She was with Sara. I see her wave from across the room and we walk towards them.

"Hi, Chloe," she says as she stands to give me a hug. "Hi," I say, smiling at both of them.

"This is Avery," I say, and Lex goes in for a hug.

"Hi. I remember you from the party," Lex says.

"This is Sara," she says introducing her to Avery. "She's, my girlfriend."

"Girlfriend?" I ask. Lex smiles shyly and gives Sara's hand a squeeze.

"I figured you would have picked up on that the last time," Lex says.

"The two of you look great together," Avery says smiling.

"Are you two..." Sara says, pointing at me and Avery, asking if we're a couple. Avery looks over at me.

"Oh, no," I say, putting my hands up.

"We're just friends." Lex looks at us and Avery looks away.

"So, Sunday funday?" I ask, changing the subject.

"Ooh, yes! I love Sunday fundays," Lex says, clapping her hands. We all order drinks and food and start discussing the trip. "You're coming with us, right?" Lex asks Avery.

"Uhm," she pauses and looks over at me.

"Maybe. I'll have to see." "Well, you should. It's going to be fun," Sara says. *I'll have to see. What's that about? She was excited about going the other night.* We look through the cabins that Lex and Sara picked out and all agree on one. We pick out dates that work for all of us before we decide to book the cabin. Two weeks from now is what we decide. We were all excited, talking about all the things we would do while we were there. We finish up our food and Lex asks if we want to continue after this. I look over at Avery, "I need to nap," she says.

"Okay. How about we all rest and after you get up, we can decide if we want to go out?" Lex asks.

"That's perfect," I say and we all part ways. We pull up to the house and Avery goes straight to the room. I follow her and she grabs clothes to change into and lays down. I proceed to do the same and sit down next to her. Her back is turned to me as she lays there quietly.

"Showering is my alone time. It's where I'm at my most vulnerable and I don't think that's something I want to share with you…yet," I say, trying not to come off rude. She doesn't say anything. "I didn't kick you out. I let you stay there," I say.

"Yeah, and then you stormed off and wouldn't even look at me," she says and turns to face me.

"You literally could've just said that, and I wouldn't have even tried to get in with you."

"I just didn't want it to turn into a fight," I say. She scoffs. "Well look at us now," she says.

"I wanted to find the right words to say. I didn't want to say anything I didn't mean because I was upset," I say.

"Whatever. And that little laugh you had when Sara tried to ask if we were together was uncalled for. It was disrespectful," she says. "Disrespectful?" I ask.

"Yes. Disrespectful," she says.

"How?" I asked with an annoyed laugh. I was starting to become irritated.

"The way you cut her off before she could even finish was mean. It made me feel like you're embarrassed of being with me," she says. "I'm not with you," I say and get off the bed.

"We're not together Avery. We've literally been talking about this all weekend." She glares at me and throws the blanket off her.

"You know what? You're right," she says as she gets out of bed and starts grabbing her things.

"What are you doing Avery?" I ask. She doesn't answer me. She continues putting her clothes in her suitcase.

"Avery. Just wait a second," I say trying to grab her.

"I'm leaving. You've made yourself pretty damn clear." she says. I have no words. I just stand there, watching her, and a few seconds later she was out the front door, and I was left standing in my room. Alone.

PART TWO

The Connection

Every part of me wanted to run after her, to stop her from leaving, but I couldn't. I physically could not get myself to move. This isn't who I am. I've never wanted to run after someone before, especially not a woman, but here I was, completely distraught at the fact that she was gone. I'm not sure how much time has passed, but I'm still standing in the same spot. *What the hell just happened. We've talked about this countless times. Was she really upset because I said we were not together, or was it the whole shower incident*? My phone dings and I rush to grab it, thinking it's Avery. Lex sent me a text.

"Want to meet at the bar when you get up?" *Fuck it. I could use a drink.*

"Ready when you are." I replied. Maybe *I can talk to them about this. I'm not sure what to do*. I change back into my clothes and leave. "Where's Avery?" Lex asks as we grab a table. "Oh, she had to head back early," I say.

"Actually, can I talk to both of you about something?" I asked her and Sara. We ordered our drinks, and I started telling them about me and Avery.

"I knew it. I could tell at the party. The way she would look at you anytime you were with Alex, I knew something was up," Lex says. I continue telling them about our talks and agreement, purposely leaving out Ivan. I don't want them judging me on that part.

"And then when I told her we weren't together, she packed her things and left. She said I had made myself clear," I say. Sara looks at Lex and then looks over at me.

"But you agreed that you would both tell each other if it became more than just hooking up right?" Lex asks.

"Yeah, we've discussed it multiple times," I say.

"Well, I think she just told you," Sara says.

"Then why would she agree with me? If she has feelings, why would she agree that it's just hooking up instead of coming out and just saying it?" I ask.

"Because if she admits it, she knows you'll cut it off. She knows it's not what you want," Lex says. She was right, I would end things with us.

"Or do you feel the same way too?" Sara asks.

"No," I said immediately. They look over at each other again. "It's not what I want. Avery and I have become good friends. If we develop feeling for each other, it'll just ruin everything."

"I hate to break it to you, but it seems like she already has," Lex says.

"It doesn't have to be a bad thing, but if you're certain that's not what you want then you need to tell her and end it before it gets worse." *That's why she brought up Ivan the other night. She's worried she may have ruined mine and Ivans friendship because of her feelings for me.* "It makes sense now," I say, not realizing it was out loud.

"What makes sense?" Lex asks.

"Oh, nothing. Let's get back to Sunday funday," I say, raising my drink.

After Lex and Sara left, I decided to go back in and have another drink. I didn't know what to think or even what to do, so I did what I knew best. I drank until I could no longer think of it anymore. It didn't help, honestly it just ended up making me think about it even more. I ordered some food since I was already there and ate to sober up a bit before heading home. It was late when I got back. Lex had texted shortly after making sure I made it home safe and letting me know that everything would work itself out. *How the hell did we get here? I tried my best to try to avoid this, and it still happened. She's going to hate me. Not only will I be losing her, but I'm also going to lose Ivan as well. Why didn't she just say something? We could have figured this out.* My phone rings and I jump. I was so lost in thought, but I snapped back quickly. I stared at my phone in disbelief, and nervously answered.

"Chloe, I'm sorry," I hear Avery's voice coming from the other side, and I'm quiet. I try to speak, but no words come out.

"Can we talk about this, please?" she asks. "I've been drinking," I say finally.

"Chloe, why do you always have to do that? Why do you always have to drink when something goes wrong?" she snaps at me. Words that I've heard, time and time again, but for some reason, this time, they hurt. My eyes began to burn, and I could feel warm tears forming. "Let's talk tomorrow. I prefer to be clear headed when we do," I say, disregarding the emotions that had overcome me, along with everything she just said.

"Go to bed. We'll talk soon," she says and hangs up. I let out a deep breath. *She was right. I always drink when something goes wrong.* I lay back on my bed and fell asleep. She doesn't call the next day, or even the day after that. *Maybe she's still trying to figure everything out too*. It's all I can think about as the days go by, and at the end of each night, I sit and wait for her call. I do know one thing though, I won't lose this friendship. I'll do anything to ensure that it works. I called Avery on Thursday evening, and she answered on the first ring.

"Hey Chloe," she says.

"Choleee, what's up? We were literally just talking about you," Ivan says right after. As always, I'm on speaker.

"Ooh, all good things I hope," I say, and we all laugh. "I'm off this weekend. We're going to Avery's parents' house on Saturday and then I'm cooking at your house Sunday," he says.

"Are you asking me or telling me?" I ask jokingly.

"I'm telling you dammit. So, cancel your plans," he says. We talked a bit about what we all want to eat so I can grab what we need from the store.

"Alright, sounds like a plan. Here's Avery. See you Sunday," he says and a few seconds later she's on the phone.

"Sorry about that. We were talking about the weekend when you called," she says.

"That's okay. It worked out perfectly," I say. We were both quiet after that, waiting for the other to speak.

"I'm sorry. I'm not sure what came over me," she says finally. "Well let's talk about it," I say.

"I overreacted. We had a good weekend, and then I overstepped Sunday morning. I may have got caught up in the moment, probably why I was in my head after brunch," she says.

"Avery, are you starting to feel something more?" I ask. She stays quiet.

"I talked to Lex and Sara and they..." She cut me off.

"You told Lex and Sara?" she asks, and I can't tell if she's upset. "Yes. I'm sorry. I just really needed someone to talk to," I say.

"Don't be sorry," she says.

"You're not mad?" I ask. "Of course not. I'm kind of glad," she says. *Glad? Maybe because I denied it at the beginning. She's distracting me.*

"You didn't answer my question," I said. "No. There's no feelings," she says after a long pause.

"I know this is causal, and somewhat of a secret, but they're your friends. You shouldn't have to hide anything from them," she says. "Okay. You still haven't explained why you flipped out on me though," I say. She laughs.

"I was in my head Chloe, that's all. I told you I would let you know if it ever happens, and it hasn't. We're fine. Anyway, I need to finish dinner. I'll see you Sunday," she says, and we hang up. *Either she's a good liar, or she actually hasn't developed feelings. If she's lying, it's just going to eat her up inside. At this point I almost want to let her deal with it on her own.* "Friends first" I hear the words in my head and roll my eyes. *I guess we'll just have to have another one of our talks. How many more of those do we have to have?* I roll over in bed and fall asleep.

Sunday gets here quickly. I was up early, getting dressed to head to the store. I always wait till the last minute, but I enjoyed a very quiet weekend alone. I walk through the grocery store, grabbing everything I need for the late lunch Ivan's making and a couple of things I need for the house. I find myself standing in the alcohol section, just staring. *Why do you always have to drink when something goes wrong?* I hear Avery's voice in my head. I walk out of the aisle empty handed. *It's Sunday, you went all weekend without drinking. What's another day?* I've never thought I had a drinking problem. I mean, I didn't drink every day. I grab a few more things and head back to the house. I'm unloading the groceries when Ivan and Avery drive up.

"You're early," I yell out as I'm walking inside. Ivan follows me in. "I need to run a few errands while I'm in town. Avery asked me to drop her off," he says.

"That's fine," I say, setting the bags on the floor.

"No beer?" he asks. "What am I? An alcoholic?" I snapped at him. He holds his hands up. "It was a joke, Chloe," he says, raising his eyebrows. "I'm sorry," I say to him, and he places a hand on my shoulder, holding me at arm's length.

"Are you okay?" he asks.

"Yeah. I'm fine," I say and smile at him. He follows me back outside and tells us he'll be back. Avery's at the trunk grabbing the rest of the bags and waves goodbye to him as she walks inside. She sets the bags down on the floor and walks over to hug me. We stayed like this for a few seconds before I let go.

"Are you okay?" I asked her.

"I am now," she says and gives me a kind smile. I really need to talk to her about everything but knowing that Ivan will be coming back makes me reconsider. I'm not exactly sure how the talk will go, and I don't want to make things awkward. We start putting up the groceries and keeping out everything that Ivan will need. We had strict orders not to start anything, he wanted to do it himself.

"How was your weekend with your parents?" I ask, trying to make conversation.

"It was good. I almost called you to come get me last night. Ivan and my dad under the same roof is so annoying," she says and we laugh. "It was good seeing my mom though. I miss our talks." I watch her face sadden for a quick second and then she snaps out of it.

"What did you do all weekend?" she asks. "I did absolutely nothing," I say laughing.

"However, I did manage to get all of my laundry done."

"I'm surprised you didn't go out," she says, and I drop everything on the counter and just look at her.

"What's that supposed to mean?" I ask and she looks at me confused.

"First Ivan, and now you? What do the two of you just sit around and talk about me drinking and going out?" I asked, annoyed. She still doesn't say anything. I turn around and walk to my room. A few minutes later she is standing in the doorway.

"Chloe, I didn't mean anything by it. What's going on?" she asked, walking towards me.

"It's nothing," I say, trying not to look at her. She grabs my hand and leads me to the bed so we can't sit down. We just sit there, and I can tell she's trying to be patient, but also wants me to talk.

"You said something the other night," I say. She sits up a little straighter and I can tell she's nervous.

"When we talked Sunday evening, you said 'Why do you always do this? Why do you always have to drink when something's wrong?' You were mad," I say.

"I was mad. Not necessarily about your drinking, well kind of about your drinking, but I was mad because I wanted to talk, and you wouldn't because you were drunk. Instead of talking about things, you drink," she says.

"Well instead of talking about things, you run" I say defensively. "Are we really going to sit here and compare defense mechanisms?" she asks, to which we both laugh.

"I didn't mean anything bad by it, but it's obviously a touchy subject for you," she says.

"I would like to think that I don't have a drinking problem, but on the other hand, I do tend to drink when something goes wrong. It's easier to forget the issues if I'm not thinking about it," I say.

"I don't care that you drink, but if something's wrong, I prefer that you call me before you grab a bottle. Okay?" she says.

"What are you, my therapist?" I ask jokingly.

"No," she says, pulling me in for a hug. "I'm your friend," she whispers in my ear.

"This is why I can't lose you Avery," I say back, and she holds me tighter.

"You never will," she says.

Ivan shows up a little while later and Avery and I sit in the kitchen as he gets things ready to cook. I heard my phone ringing and went over to grab it. It was Lex.

"Hey Lex," I say, walking back into the kitchen. We talked for a few minutes and then she reminded me about the trip.

"Oh, we leave Friday, don't we?" I asked excitedly.

"Good thing I finished my laundry this weekend." I look over at Avery.

"Okay, see you then" I say and hang up.

"Where are you going?" Ivan asks.

"We have a girls trip this weekend," I say.

"Oh damn, that's happening this weekend? That came fast," he says.

"Have you done your laundry, babe?" he asks Avery and laughs. *She told him. I wasn't sure if she had since we had been fighting. Was it fighting? We haven't actually fought, have we?*

"What time are you leaving?" Ivan asks. "Friday morning. We'll be back Monday night," I say.

"I hate both of you. What am I supposed to do all weekend?" he asks.

"Get some friends," Avery says, and we burst into laughter.

"I have friends. I have Chloe," he says, and we laugh again.

"If you keep laughing at me, neither one of you are getting any of this food," he says, trying to keep a serious face. We settle down and try to catch our breath. We continue to talk about the trip while Ivan finishes the food. Avery says that she'll wait until Ivan gets home

Thursday and then she'll head over here that night. She lets him know that she'll either head home Monday night when we get back, or she'll leave Tuesday morning, depending on how tired she is. When we get done eating, Avery volunteers to clean up the kitchen and Ivan and I head outside and sit on the porch swing. We sit there for a while, both in food comas, when I feel him turn to look at me. My eyes were closed, and my head was leaning back.

"Why are you staring at me?" I ask, not opening my eyes. "How do you do that?" he asks, and I smile. I lean forward and turn to look at him.

"What's up?" I ask. "Are you okay?" he asks, and I roll my eyes. "Chole, I'm serious. You seem like you've been in your head a lot recently, don't think I haven't noticed. And you snapped at me earlier. What the hell was that about?" he asks. *I've been in my head so much because your girlfriend stresses me out.*

"Are you still thinking about..." he pauses.

"HER?" he asks. I give him an 'are you seriously asking me that?' kind of look.

"Want me to whoop his ass?" he asks, grinning from ear to ear. "Whoop who's ass?" Avery asks, walking out of the back door.

"That Alex guy. I told Chloe I would whoop his ass," he says. "Why?" she asks, looking at me.

"Are you talking to him again?" She looks pissed.

"No, I'm not talking to him again. And I don't need you to whoop his ass," I say to Ivan. Him and Avery look over at each other.

"Well, whatever it is, you can always talk about it. With either one of us," Ivan says.

"We love you. Right Avery?" he asks, grabbing her hand. She looks over at me and smiles.

"We're here for you," she says, doing a good job of avoiding the *love* part.

"We should have a movie night," Ivan says jumping up. Avery and I look at each other.

"We can go to the store, get snacks and all lay in the living room and watch a movie," he pauses and looks over at me.

"We could build a fort," he says.

"A fort?" Avery asks curiously.

"Yeah. Chloe and I used to build forts all the time when we were younger. Right Chloe?" he asks, and I look over at Avery.

"We used to build forts when one of us was going through something, and sit there and talk for hours," I say. I look over at Ivan and smile.

"So, let's do it!" he says.

Later that evening, Ivan goes to the store for snacks and leaves Avery and I in charge of getting the living room ready for movie night. We start moving furniture around and grabbing all the blankets and pillows I own.

"I can't believe you and Ivan used to do stuff like this," she says. "He always did stuff like this for me," I say, and she looks at me questioningly.

"He made it a point to do everything he could to make me feel better," I say. I look up at her and shake my head, as if I'm telling her not to ask about it, and she doesn't. We continue setting up the living room and I can tell she's lost in thought. I wrap my arm around her waist and turn her around to face me.

"Stop thinking about it," I say. She shakes her head.

"I wasn't." I give her a knowing look.

"Okay fine, but what did you..." I pull her in for a kiss before she can finish her question. I kiss her softly and passionately, trying to make her forget whatever it was she wanted to ask. I pull back and look at her as she focuses on me. I watch as the lust pools in her eyes, a look that I'm all too familiar with. She moves in closer and just before our lips meet, I whisper, "We should finish." She leans her forehead against mine and laughs. We build the fort against one of the couches, leaving the front part open so we can see the T.V. Ivan walks in just as we're finishing and his eyes light up like a child. "Bad ass," he says, nodding his head in appreciation. We crawl into the fort and Ivan dumps out all the snacks. He looks at Avery as he goes to sit down.

"Babe, let me sit in the middle please?" he asks her, and she scoots over. He throws an arm around both of us.

"This is perfect," he says, looking over at her and then over at me. I feel a sudden rush of peace come over me and lay my head on his shoulder. *This is perfect.* The next few days seem to fly right by. Thursday morning, I received a text from Lex asking to meet for lunch. We agreed to meet at a café downtown instead of our usual spot.

"I'm so excited for this weekend. Oh, Sara and I are leaving this evening when she gets off work. We wanted to make sure everything was good to go," Lex says.

"You mean the two of you are leaving this evening so you can be alone the first night?" I ask, teasing her. She blushes.

"Okay, yeah," she says, and we laugh.

"Well not to worry, Avery and I didn't plan to take off until tomorrow morning," I say, and she raises and eyebrow.

"Avery huh. I was wondering if she was going to come or not," she says.

"Yeah, we're good now. She's coming down tonight, after she gets off work," I say.

"I guess we'll both have fun tonight," she says with an excited look on her face.

"Oh, hush," I say, nudging her.

"Are you almost done? I have to get back to work," I say. I head back to the office to finish up a few things before I leave for the weekend. Avery sent me a message to let me know she got off work early and she was going home to finish packing. I had everything ready and decided to order dinner before I left work, hoping it would be ready by the time Avery arrived. We pulled up to the house at the same time. "Did you just get off work?" Avery asked as she got out of her car. I opened the front door, letting her in first since she had her luggage. "Yes," I say once we finally settle in.

"I wanted to fish a few things before we left, and I grabbed dinner."

"Oh, great. I'm starving. I made Ivan dinner before I left so he would have it when he got home, but I didn't want to eat," she says.

"Wow, your last night in town and you bail on him for dinner?" I say, shaking my head in disapproval.

"Stop," she says laughing. "He's been guilt tripping me all week. If I had stayed for dinner I would have given in and stayed home. I'm excited to go on this trip. I got off early so I could get things done and get on the road," she says.

"He's a grown man," I say, walking past her to grab some plates. "He'll live." I set the plates down and serve us so we can eat. I can tell she's deep in thought. *I wonder if she's having second thoughts about going*. I placed my hand on her shoulder, trying to grab her attention.

"What?" she asks. "I asked if you would like a glass of wine," I said.

"Oh, yeah. That sounds good," she says, trying to focus. "Sit down. I'll grab it." She gets up and pours each of us a glass.

"If you think it will be a problem, you don't have to come, Avery," I finally say.

"It's not that. It's nothing," she says. *I wonder if she's as nervous as I am. We hang out all the time, but we've never been alone. Not like this*.

"Now who's in their head?" she asks jokingly. "Can we eat now, please?" We make small talk while we eat. I told her I had lunch with Lex earlier, and she told me more about Ivan and his guilt tripping. I pick up our plates when we're done and head to my room to find something more comfortable to change into.

"Hey, Avery," I called out from the room. "I'm going to take a quick shower."

"Okay," she says from behind me, wrapping her arms around my waist. I jump and try not to scream.

"Why do you do that?" I say laughing.

"Thank you for inviting me," she says, still holding me.

"You're welcome," I say, giving her a quick kiss on the cheek. "Now move," I say and before I leave the room, I turn to look at her. "By the way, I'm happy you're coming with me."

We wake up early the next morning, getting everything ready before we take off.

"So, are Lex and Sara meeting us there?" she asks, as we're loading the car up.

"Oh, they left yesterday after Sara got off work," I say smiling so she'll get the hint.

"Lucky them," I hear her say under her breath and I smile at the thought. We grab the rest of our things and head to the gas station. Avery goes in to pay while I pump the gas.

"I got snacks," she says holding up the bag. I get back in the care and look over at her.

"Ready to be stuck with me for the next four days?" I asked and gave her a wicked smile.

"I think the real question is, are you ready to be stuck with me?" she says, returning the playful smile. We're on the road for the next five hours. I watched Avery eat all our snacks as we sang ridiculously loud, at the top of our lungs, and we talked about any and everything. The closer we got, the more the scenery began to change. We could finally see the mountains. I could tell how in awe she was at the colors of the trees.

"It's beautiful, isn't it?" I ask, looking over at her. She was smiling as she gazed out of the window.

"I've never seen anything like it," she says, and we drive in silence. We had about an hour left of our drive when Lex called.

"Hey, Chloe. How far away are you?" she asks.

"We have a little under an hour to go," I say. "Perfect. I'm going to make reservations at a restaurant so we can eat when you arrive. It'll give you enough time to unpack," she says.

"And change," Avery yells out.

"Yes. I figured you'd dress comfy for the drive," Lex says.

"See you soon Lex," I say, and we hang up.

"I hope she picks something good. I'm starving," I say. Avery gives me a surprised look and leans over to grab the bag.

"I bought snacks," she says. She opens the bag and then sets it down slowly.

"Yeah, and you ate them all," I say. We looked at each other and immediately started laughing. We turn down the long winding road with tall trees that cover the street. In the distance, we can start to see the cabins. I was so excited, and I could tell Avery was as well.

"Wow," I hear her say quietly as we pull into the driveway. I sent Lex a message, letting her know we had arrived and a few seconds later she and Sara were on the porch. We got out of the car and grabbed our luggage. Lex guides us inside, giving us a tour of the house. The cabin was beautiful. It consisted of two levels. The bottom level had your usual kitchen, living room area, a beautiful bedroom and a huge patio in the back. There was a bar-b-que pit, a hot tub, and a built-in fireplace in the center. The upper level had a small living room area connected with a bedroom and bathroom. There was an incredible wall of windows with a sliding door that led to a small deck outside. The view from the deck was amazing. I stood there for a minute, taking it all in.

"This room is yours," I hear Lex say from behind me. I turn to face her, and she smiles.

"Consider it a thank you for helping me pick it out." I give her hand a quick squeeze.

"Now, I know it's beautiful, but we need to get dressed. Dinner is at 7," she says and leaves the room.

"What do you think?" I ask Avery as I walk up behind her. She turns around and hugs me.

"This is...," she pauses. "I know," I say as I let her go. "Come on. Let's get dressed."

We arrived at the restaurant with a few minutes to spare. It was a nice place, not extremely fancy, and sat right on the edge of a lake. They sat us at a more private table, in the back near the windows. We could see out to the back patio, it was cool out, so I was glad they sat us inside. We all settled in and started looking over the menu.

"How was the drive?" Lex asked, making small talk.

"It was good. We took the scenic route," I say, smiling down at my menu.

"Smooth Chloe," Lex says, giving me a knowing look. Avery looks over at me.

"Wait, you've been here before?" she asks, and it sounds like she's upset.

"Of course, she has. When I told her about the trip, and when she found out about me and Sara, she recommended it," Lex says. "Well, thank you. It's lovely here, and I'm glad the two of you agreed to join us," Sara says smiling. "So, it wasn't actually a girl's trip?" Avery asks, confused.

"Well, it started off that way," Lex says.

"But Lex wanted to 'woo' Sara, so I helped her," I say, and we laugh. I reach under the table, placing my hand on Avery's lap, trying to relax her. I could tell she was trying to take everything in, and I didn't want her over thinking anything. The waiter comes over and we order our food and a bottle of wine. We talk over dinner and when we're done, we make our way to the patio to check out the view. I walk over to Avery as she stands behind the railing, staring out into the darkness.

"This place is pretty nice, isn't it?" I ask, standing next to her. "I'm sure it isn't your first time here," she says in a monotone voice. Before I get the chance to respond, Lex walks over to us.

"I stocked the fridge with drinks earlier today. I think it's time to get this party started," she says, gleaming.

"Yes! I'm ready for another drink," Avery says. Lex shoots me a questioning look over her shoulder and I just shrug. At this moment, I was glad we all decided to take one car. I didn't want to have a silent ride back to the cabin. When we arrived, we all agreed to change into more comfortable clothes. Avery and I headed upstairs and before she walked into the bathroom, I grabbed her hand to stop her.

"Avery. We're not doing this. This is supposed to be a fun weekend. So, what's going on?" I ask calmly. She turned to look at me. "Do you bring all the girls you sleep with here?" she asks and immediately looks ashamed for even asking. I was shocked. I really could not believe she asked me that. She lets out a slight chuckle.

"Wow. I should have known. I figured things would be different now because we were more than just two people hooking up. We were friends. Or at least I thought we were," she says. She grabs her clothes and walks into the bathroom to change. *What the hell was that*? I was completely taken aback. I hear her coming out of the bathroom and push her right back in, closing the door behind us. Her eyes widened.

"Chloe, what the hell," she says.

"Listen to me Avery. I've never brought anyone here before, not romantically, or any other way. This is my favorite place to be. I would never ruin it by bringing just anyone. And this *is* different," I say, grabbing her hands.

"You're my favorite person. And if I'm being completely honest, I've never taken a girl anywhere, but to bed. I've been doing a lot of firsts with you, but your tantrums are making them very hard to be enjoyable." I had never talked to her like that before and I could tell she was just as shocked as I was. I hold out my hand and watch as she hesitates to take it. I pull her in for a hug, almost as if I was apologizing.

"Now, can we go get drunk?" I asked, smiling at her. She kisses me on the cheek and runs downstairs as I stay back, grabbing clothes to change. I throw some water on my face and take a deep breath.

"Chloe! Get your ass down here!" I hear Lex yell from downstairs. She meets me at the bottom of the staircase and hands me a shot. "To our weekend getaway," she raises her glass and turns to see Sara and Avery with their glasses raised as well. We spent the next few hours drinking, laughing, and dancing around the kitchen. As midnight rolls around, we decided to call it a night so we could have some kind of energy for the next day. We all said goodnight and Avery and I walked up to the room. She plops down on the bed and laughs.

"I think I'm drunk," she says and sits up.

"Come lay down." "I'm going to shower first," I say and make my way to the bathroom to turn on the water. Once it gets warm enough, I start to undress when I hear the door open.

"Prove to me this is different," I hear her say in a low voice as she walks towards me. She stands behind me, running her hands down my arms. She moves my hair to one side and plants gentle kisses on my shoulder.

"Please, Chloe." I slide the shower door open and step in slowly.

After a second or two I look back at her and ask "Are you coming?" She smiles at me and starts to undress. We were lying in bed, and I was more asleep than awake. Avery was laying on her side, running her fingers through my hair and caressing my face as she always does when we finish.

"Chloe. Are you awake?" she asks quietly. I was too tired to answer, so to avoid any questions, I just lay there with my eyes closed. "Chloe," I hear her say again. "I love you."

I wake up before her the next morning and try my best not to wake her. *Was I dreaming? Did she really say that*? I felt a sudden rush of adrenaline as I began to think more about it. *Was this excitement*? *Was I excited at the thought of her loving me*? I roll out of bed as quietly as possible to wash up and head downstairs to make a cup of coffee.

I see that Lex had already beat me to it. "Want some?" she asks quietly.

"Please," I say walking over to her. "Is Sara still asleep?"

"Yeah, I didn't want to wake her up," she says. "Is Avery asleep too?" I nod as she hands me my cup.

"Ooh, wild night?" she asks, nudging my arm. I look over at her. "Oh shit. Let's go out to the patio," she says. We get the fire going and share a blanket on one of the couches.

"Okay. Let me hear it," she says as she settles in. I tell her everything that happened when we got up to the room, sparing her a few details, of course.

"And then I'm pretty sure she told me that she loved me," I say. She stays quiet.

"I could have been dreaming though, or maybe I was just really drunk," She looks at me.

"None of us were that drunk," she says as I stare into the fire. "I mean, would it be a bad thing?" she asks. *Would it be*? I've never cared much about how nay woman felt about me. If they fell in love, then that's something they would have to deal with. Alone. But Avery.... The thought of her of her falling in love with me, scared me, until I heard her say it. I shake the warm feeling that I was beginning to feel in my chest. I still haven't told Lex about Ivan, and I didn't plan on doing so either. She reaches out and grabs my hand.

"Everything that's meant to be will always fall into place," she says. We heard the back door open and turned to see Sara and Avery standing in the doorway.

"Come sit with us," Lex calls out.

"Bring another blanket." She gave my hand one last squeeze and moved to the other couch to sit with Sara. Avery walks towards me and I lift the blanket so she can sit down.

"Good morning," I say and give her a kind smile. She smiles back at me and scoots in. I don't know what to say to her and try my best not to make it awkward. I'm still not even one hundred percent sure she said it. I place my hand on her leg under the cover and she puts her hand on mine.

"Should we cook or go grab breakfast?" Lex asks.

"We should get dressed and go out," I say.

"Yeah!" Sara says. "Then we can go downtown or something. See where the day takes us," I say. Everyone agrees and we make our way back inside. I got upstairs and started looking through my bags to find something to wear. Avery walks over to me and starts looking through her bags too.

"How did you sleep?" Avery asks, avoiding eye contact.

"Good. I don't even remember falling asleep," I say. She stays quiet.

"Should we dress up or wear something comfortable? I don't think it's going to get any warmer outside," I say. She leans over and reaches into my bag, pulling out a pair of leggings and a sweater.

"Here, this will work," she says. I look at the clothes she laid out on the bed.

"Don't worry," she says, grabbing her clothes and heading into the bathroom.

"You look good in anything." She smiles and closes the door behind her. We all meet downstairs and in the kitchen after we finish getting dressed. I was pleased to see that we all chose to dress comfortably for the day.

"I looked up places to eat near downtown and found a nice little café on the strip," Sara says.

"Perfect," I say.

Lex grabs the keys, and we head out. About half an hour later we pulled up to the café and went inside.

"This place is so cute," Lex says as we walk over to a booth and sit down. The waitress walks over to us and takes our drink orders as we look over the menu. Avery and I decided on two different plates so we can share since they looked good. "That's cute. The two of you are cute,"

Lex says and looks over at Sara. "Why can't we be cute like that?" she asks pouting.

"Because you don't like to share," Sara says, and we laugh. Our food comes out quick and we eat more than we talk.

"Damn I guess we were all hungry," I say.

"Don't worry, we'll walk it all off on the strip." I slid out of the booth and paid for our food.

"Thanks for breakfast," Lex says, throwing her arm around me as we walk out.

"Have you asked her yet?" Lex asks.

"Lex!" I say quietly, jabbing my elbow into her side.

"Don't be so loud."

"Don't worry, she's bonding with Sara," she says as we continue walking.

"I haven't asked her. I'm not even sure how to ask her. I think she wanted to bring it up this morning, but I changed the subject," I say.

"Really Chloe?" she asks.

"I got nervous," I say laughing.

"Nervous about what?" I heard Avery say from behind me and I turned to face her.

"Oh, nothing," I say, hooking my arm into hers.

"Come on. I want to take you to this cute souvenir store." We walk down the block, still arm in arm, and I look back at Lex and Sara. They looked so cute together, just walking, laughing, and enjoying being out together. We were a few steps ahead of them and I called out to Lex,

"Hey! We're going in here," I say pointing to the store. She gave me a thumbs up and we walked in. We looked around the store at all the clothes and keychains they had.

"Should I get something for Iv..." Avery says, and I cut her off. "What?" she asks. I looked around to see where Lex and Sara were. They were standing a few feet away from us looking at matching sweaters. I look back at Avery, who's still looking at me confused.

"Lex doesn't know about Ivan," I say quietly. She looks shocked. "Are you serious?" she asks.

"I didn't want her to judge me," I say.

"She knows you though, Chloe. They all know you only hook up with girls that are in relationships," she says.

"Don't say it like that. It sounds ugly," I say, disgusted.

"Well, it's true," she says.

"Okay, well Ivan isn't just some random guy. He's my best friend," I say. She rolls her eyes at me and walks away.

"Fuck," I say under my breath, and she walks back towards me. "Ivan is nobody," she says and my jaw drops.

"At least not while we're here. Now let's go find matching shirts and continue being cute like they say we are," she says and pulls me towards Lex and Sara. We find shirts that match their sweaters and go to the register to pay.

"These are so cute," Lex squeals. "We can wear them and take a group picture at the cabin." I roll my eyes at her and Avery and Sara laugh. We continued to walk down the strip, stopping at a few stores and window shopping at others. For lunch, we stop at a small diner to eat and rest our legs.

"I love these little 'hole in the wall' restaurants," Sara says. "They always have the best service and food."

"Should we continue walking around or should we do something else?" Lex asks as we enjoyed our meal. We all looked at each other, waiting to see who would speak first.

"I have an idea. There's a nice lake here. It's surrounded by trees and mountains. They have a couple things there to do as well," I say. "That sounds fun," Avery says and looks at Sara and Lex for agreement. "We can head over there when we're done here," I say, and we continue talking and eating. We walked back to the car. Avery and I are still arm in arm as we had been since we arrived.

"You're going to love this place. It's so pretty. I try to go every time I come up here," I say to Avery. The drive is about forty-five minutes. I watch Lex and Sara through the rear-view mirror as we get closer. They're both staring out of their windows, looking up at the trees and mountains. Avery reaches for my hand and smiles at me. With her hand still in mine, I point out the window, so she'll see the deer on the side of the road.

"Look, I see the lake," I hear Sara telling Lex as we get closer. When we finally parked, I let them know that it may be colder here, but I had a couple of blankets in the trunk. We walk down to the sand, and I watch them all stand there in admiration. A light fog hung over the lake, making it impossible to enjoy the activities. We were all running around in the sand, laughing like children, and in that moment time stopped. I watched Avery as she was smiling with no care in the world, and I felt this jolt of happiness run through my body. I stood there, unable to take my eyes off of her. The warm feeling in my chest this morning had suddenly taken over my whole body. I knew everything was about to change. But in that very moment, as I stood there, watching her, hearing only the sound of her laughter, I knew that I loved her too.

We got back to the cabin early that afternoon. We were all tired and cold and decided we would go back to warm up and relax.

"I think we're going to take a nap," Lex tells me as we're walking through the front door.

"Sounds like a good idea," I say as I watch Avery walk up the stairs. She's changing when I walk into the room.

"Do you want to change and take a nap with me?" she asks sleepily and crawls into bed. I smile, nod my head, and go find some sweats to change into. We lay on our sides, staring at each other, not saying a word.

"Turn around," I say quietly and pull her into me when she does. I wasn't tired, but I laid there until she fell asleep anyway. I grabbed a blanket and quietly went out the sliding door onto the deck. I wrapped myself up and sat on one of the chairs. I stared out into the trees and started thinking about Avery. *How long have I felt like this, or am I just feeling it because she said it? Either way, it will not end well since she's with Ivan.* "Fuck…Ivan," I hear my self say in a low voice. *What the hell am I going to do*? After sitting out there for a while, I feel my phone vibrate. It was a text from Lex.

"Are you asleep?" I read as I heard the back door to the patio shut slowly. I go back inside, and tiptoe through the room. I walk out of the back door, still wrapped in my blanket, and sit next to Lex. She had the fire pit started and a blanket over her legs.

"Did you take a nap?" I asked her. "I'm too excited to sleep. I don't want to waste my time here napping," she says.

"What about you?" I take a deep breath and watch the fire.

"No, I didn't sleep. I couldn't sleep. I think I love her too," I say. "You think?" she asks.

"Okay. I do," I say and turn to face her. She's smiling ear to ear as if I just told *her* I was in love with her and I laugh.

"Well, are you going to tell her?" she asks.

"At some point," I say, and she glares at me.

"Let's go get them up. I made dinner plans," I say. I go up to our room and find Avery still asleep. I go through my bag and pull out the black dress I brought for dinner and the dress that Avery wore to my birthday party. The one she mistakenly left behind when she ran out on me the following morning. I take a quick shower and when I walk out, I see Avery awake, holding the dress.

"What's this?" she asks, holding the dress up.

"Your dress," I say smiling, knowing she'll roll her eyes at me. "Why do you have it?" she proceeds.

"We're going to dinner tonight. I wasn't sure if you had packed one, so I brought it. You left it at the house," I say.

"Right," she says looking down. I walk over to her and sit next to her on the bed.

"When did you wake up?" she asks, changing the subject.

"I didn't sleep," I say, and she lifts her head. "I wasn't tired. Plus, I needed to make this dinner reservation. So, get up," I say, smacking her leg.

"Let's get dressed."

"Where are we going anyway?" Avery asks from the shower. "It's a restaurant my family, and I go to when we're all here. The food is amazing," I say, trying not to give too much away. Avery's finishing up in the bathroom and I sneak downstairs.

"Damn, Chloe," I hear Lex say when I reach the bottom step. "Tell Avery she can go with Sara. I'm going with you," she says as she admires me from the counter.

"Hey," Sara says, smacking Lex on the arm.

"You do look really pretty though." We're all laughing around the table when I see Lex look up and nod in the direction of the staircase. I turn around to see Avery and she freezes. I raise an eyebrow and give her a quick smile before turning back around.

"Avery, can I have your date?" Lex asks jokingly. "No way in hell," she says and kisses my shoulder.

"You look…" she pauses as her eyes begin to wonder.

"Okay, that's enough," I say, putting my hands up.

"Let's go, I don't want to be late."

"Are you at least going to give us a little hint as to where we're going?" Lex asks on the way to the restaurant. I stay quiet and look at her through the rearview mirror.

"It must be fancy. Look how we're dressed," Sara says. We go deeper into the hills, and I see Lex look slightly nervous.

"Wait, are we lost? The city is back that way," she says and again I say nothing. I make one final turn that goes straight into the parking lot.

"Woah," I hear Avery say and Lex and Sara lean forward to see out of the front window.

"My family and I come to dinner here every time we make a trip," I say as I park the car. We walked inside and I let them know I had a reservation for Chloe. They lead us to our table, and we sit as I watch them admire the place.

"I see why you asked us to dress up now," Lex says. The restaurant was more 'upper class', so to speak. The waiter came over to us with our menus and I told him to start us off with a bottle of wine. "There's an upstairs area?" Sara asks.

"Yes. It's a bar. Strictly for those who come to eat. I have a table waiting for us when we're done here," I say.

"Chloe, you didn't have to do all this," Lex says. "I thought it would be nice for the two of you. You've been a really good friend to me, Lex, one of the best I've had. This is my way of thanking you," I say. She gives my hand a tight squeeze and I return it.

"Now, let's order our food so we can get up there."

We spent the next hour or so enjoying our meal and talking about the trip so far.

"The city is so beautiful," Avery says.

"Yeah, we used to come up here at least twice a year, but we haven't been back in a while," I say. The waiter comes up to us to clear the table and lets me know everything is ready for us upstairs. They keep the lights dim at the bar because the walls are all made of glass. You can see a perfect view of the city down below that gives the place its glorious lighting. We were heading towards our table when suddenly I heard a familiar voice.

"I had to see it to believe it." I turn around instantly at the sound of his voice, and he pulls me into his arms and spins me around.

"Hi," I say laughing. He puts me down but keeps his arms around me.

"It's been a while," he says smiling, not breaking eye contact. We stay that way for a moment as if we were both watching the past in each other's eyes.

"Where's the family?" he asks, finally looking away, searching the room.

"Oh, I'm actually here with some friends," I say, pointing towards our table. I realize they are all staring at us, and I let go of him quickly.

"Come, I'll introduce you," I say and lead him to the table. "Ladies, this is Andres," I say as we stand in front of the table.

"Andres, these are my friends Lex, Sara," I pause, setting my hand on Avery's shoulder, "and this is Avery." She freezes when I touch her, but I don't react.

"It's very nice to meet you all," he says, giving them a flashy smile. "I'll get you girls some drinks."

"I'll come with you," I say, and we head over to the bar. I can see the girls all looking at one another, but I can't tell what they're saying. Andres walks behind the bar and holds out a bottle of wine.

"Is it still your favorite?" he asks.

"Of course. I didn't think you would remember," I say.

"It hasn't been that long," he says. He grabs some glasses, and we head back to the table. He pulls my chair out for me, and I sit down, noticing that Avery scoots away from me slowly. He pours each of us a glass, glancing down at me every time he sets a glass down.

"You should have a drink with us," I say, looking up at him. "I have work to do," he says.

"If you're still here when I get done, I'll come and have a glass. He gives my shoulder a quick squeeze and walks away.

"Okay, who is *he*?" Lex finally asks and I can practically feel Avery roll her eyes.

"His parents own the restaurant. After coming here for quite some time, our parents became friends and we'd hang out when I was here," I say. Lex stares at me as if she thinks I'm keeping something from her.

"There's no dirt. Don't try to make something out of nothing," I say and laugh. We continued with our night, enjoying our wine. Andres signals me over a little later. He was standing with his parents, and I walked over to greet them. We stood there talking for a few minutes and when I headed back to the table, I noticed that the girls were gone. I look around the room and see Lex and Sara mingling with a few people and then I see Avery over in the corner, staring out over the city. I walk over to her, she looks deep in thought, trying to mask it as if she's taking in the view. I stand next to her for a minute before she realized I'm there. "Hi," I say, linking my arm into hers. She looks back out of the window but doesn't stop me.

"Avery, I need to tell you something," I say, turning her towards me. She stands there, looking down at her wine.

"I heard you last night," I say. She looks up at me, half afraid and half worried.

She begins to shake her head, "Chloe, I'm sorry," she pauses and looks back down. Before she can say anything else, I grab her hand and cut her off.

"I love you too," I say. She looks up at me again, this time with a shocked look on her face.

"What?" she asks and her voice cracks. I step closer to her, still holding her hand.

"I love you, Avery," I say again. She smiles, gently grabs my face, and kisses me. I place my hand on hers and smile. Suddenly her touch sent shock waves down my body. This felt….different. I gave her one more kiss before we walked back over to Lex and Sara, hand in hand. I nod at Lex and she gives me a caring smile and squeezes my free hand.

"Should we head back to the house?" Lex asks, and we all agree. "Let me go say my goodbye's. I'll meet you at the car," I say and hand Lex the keys. I watch them walk downstairs and scan the room, trying to find Andres.

"Hey, we're taking off already," I say when I find him.

"I'll walk you outside," he says, holding out his arm. We say goodbye as we stand in each other's arms for a few seconds.

"She's a lucky girl. I hope she knows that" he whispers in my ear. I look up at him and smile as he kisses my forehead.

"Come back soon, please," he says, and I walk towards the car.

Back at the cabin, we all go into our rooms for the night. I'm standing in the bathroom, washing my face, when Avery walks in. She stands behind me, wraps her arms around me and sets her chin on my shoulder. We stand like this for a minute, staring at each other in the mirror.

"You love me too," she says quietly and smiles. I smile back at her and nod my head. I grabbed her hand and led her to the small couch on the other side of the room. We grab a blanket and sit together staring out into the night.

"I was nervous," Avery said quietly. Her back was facing me as she was leaning on me on the couch.

"About what?" I asked, rubbing my hand up and down her forearm.

"When you said that you heard me last night. I didn't know what to say, or how to react," she says. I let out a small laugh and she turns slightly to face me.

"I'm serious," she says, trying to hold in her laugh. Her smile slowly fades as her eyes begin to water. I sit up on the couch, pulling her up with me.

"I thought I was going to lose you," she says. The quiver in her voice sends chills down my spine. I wipe away the tears from her face and pull her closer towards me. I stay quiet, thinking of the way I felt this morning when I woke up.

"I was nervous too. Honestly, I thought about it all day," I say. "Why didn't you say anything?" she asks as she leans forward and sits opposite of me on the couch. "I didn't know what to say. I think I may have been in a state of shock. I even told Lex," I say.

"You told Lex?" she asks.

"Yes. I'm sorry. I needed to talk about it," I say. She laughs and I look at her confused. *Is she not mad?*

"I told Sara when we were walking down the strip," she says. I smile at her and look down at my hands.

"Then what happened?" she asks. I could tell she wanted to know everything that led me to saying it back.

"We were at the lake," I say. She nods her head as if she were telling me to continue. I look away from her, trying not to smile. "Chole!" she says impatiently. I smile and shake my head.

"When we were at the lake, running around in the sand, I looked over at you. You had the biggest smile on your face and the only sound I could hear was the sound of your laughter." Her eyes began to water again as I continued to explain.

"I guess at that moment, I just knew." She grabbed my hand and led me towards the bed. Everything from the way she touched me, to the way she kissed me had become even more passionate than before. *Is this what it was like to be in love with a woman? Or, was this what it was like to be in love with Avery?*

It was our last full day at the cabin. We sat around the kitchen table having breakfast and talking about how much we've enjoyed our time here.

"So, I hope you don't mind, but I've planned a whole day for Sara and I," Lex says.

"Of course not," I say. "Yeah, the two of you deserve a day to yourselves," Avery says. Lex looks over at us suspiciously.

"You did the same thing, didn't you?" Lex asks. I smile and wink at her as I take a sip of my coffee.

"Okay, well if you want to meet for dinner, or just meet back here tonight, let me know," I say to Lex as I clean up mine and Avery's plates. She's lying in bed when I get back up to the room and I join her. "Would you be upset if I said I didn't want to go out today?" she asks softly. I scoot closer to her, and she wraps her arm around me.

"Not at all," I say, and we lay there silently together as we both fall asleep. It was midday when I finally woke up. I turn around and see that Avery's not next to me and I get out of bed.

"Avery?" I call out, thinking she may have gone downstairs, but I get no response. As I get closer to the staircase, I can hear her talking very faintly. I walk over to the sliding doors and step out onto the deck. I could hear her out on the patio, but I didn't look out over the railing. "I miss you too, I'll be home tomorrow," I hear her say. *She's talking to Ivan.*

"Fuck…Ivan," I say in a low voice as I think about the events of the past two days. I make my way back into the room, quietly closing the door so she doesn't hear me. I grab some clothes and go into the bathroom to shower. I'm standing there, lost in thought, when I hear a knock at the door that startles me.

"Chloe?" I hear Avey say. "In the shower," I call out, wondering how long I've been in here.

"Why did you lock the door?" she asks.

"Out of habit, sorry," I say, knowing I just needed a few minutes to myself. "I'll be out in a minute." She's standing at the sliding doors when I walk out of the bathroom and turns to look at me. *She looks pissed*.

"Is everything okay?" she asks as she walks towards me.

"Yes," I say and continue to put my clothes back into my bag. "Why did you lock the door?" she asks again.

"It was just out of habit," I say, turning to look at her. "I think I should be the one asking *you* if everything is okay." She looks clueless. I finish putting my things away and notice that she hasn't moved. When I look over at her she has tears rolling down her face.

"Avery," I say, stepping towards her. I cup her face in my hands, wiping her tears.

"What's going on?" I ask. She pulls my hands away from her face and holds them in hers.

"What am I going to do?" she asks quietly and sobs.

"What do you mean?" I ask and lead her towards the couch so we can sit down.

"Because I'm in love with you. What am I supposed to do?" She asks.

"Don't worry about that. We'll figure it out," I say, wiping another tear from her face. I pulled her into my arms and held her. The truth was, I wasn't sure what we were going to do. I was always careful about these things, but somewhere along the line, I had let my guard down. I was in love with my best friend's girlfriend, and I had no idea how I was going to handle this. The last thing I wanted to do was show Avery that I was just as worried as she was.

"Let's not worry about it right now, okay?" I said.

"How about I run you a bath and we can figure out how we want to spend our last day here," I say. She nods her head and walks over to her bag to grab some clothes. I get the bath ready for her and once she's calmed down a bit, she gets in. I give her some space, grab my phone off the dresser and step out onto the deck. I stare out into the trees and all I can think about is Ivan. I hated the fact that I put myself in this situation, but I didn't regret the way I felt about her. *He's going to hate me.* I needed someone to talk to. I couldn't talk to Ivan, obviously, and I didn't want to ruin Lex and Sara's day. Andres. Other than Ivan, Andres was the only other person that knew everything about me. I decided to give him a call.

"Hey, Chloe," he says when he picks up.

"Hi, is this a good time?" I ask.

"Of course. What's going on?" he says. I let out a deep breath. "I need your advice," I say, and he laughs.

"You want my advice?" he asks. I stay quiet. *Maybe this was a bad idea.*

"Okay, what's up?" he says. I give him the 'long story short' version of everything that's been going on.

"Shit, Chloe," he says.

"I know. Please don't make me feel worse," I say.

"What would you do if it was you?" I asked him.

"You mean if I was you, or if I was him?" he asks.

"If you were Ivan," I say. There was a long silence on the phone, I could tell he was thinking.

"Do you want the honest truth," he says, finally.

"Please," I say in a begging voice.

"I'd be pissed," he says. I wince at the thought.

"But I'd understand." I was shocked.

"What?" I ask. "I would understand. If he knows you the way you say he does, then he'll understand. You're special Chloe, you always have been. It's hard to know you and not love everything about you. Everyone that comes into your life has to know their place with you, or they'll lose you. I've seen it happen. So, trust me. He'll get it," he says. I stayed quiet, I didn't know what to say.

"Look, I have to get back to work. Don't overthink it okay," he says. "Thank you, Andres. I needed that," I say.

"You're one of a kind, Chloe. Don't ever forget that," he says. I smile and hang up the phone.

We decided to go to town for a late lunch and I can tell Avery's still thinking about everything, as was I.

"What do you feel like doing after this?" I asked her as I pushed my food around the plate.

"Can we go back to the lake? It's pretty outside, maybe we can get on the pedal boats this time," she says. *The lake. Could it be because she knows that's the place it all clicked for me, or does she actually want to go pedal boating?*

"Of course, we can," I say. It really was a pretty day. The skies were clear and there was just enough of a breeze to keep it cool outside. We got on the pedal boat, and I let Avery take control. It took her a few times to get it down as we laughed, but once she finally gets the hang of it, we're quiet again. I don't want to say anything about the situation, I want to enjoy the ride on the lake.

"It's so nice to actually enjoy fall," Avery says as she looks around at all the trees.

"The leaves back home don't change color like they do here." "You should see them during spring," I say.

"Will you show me? I mean if we're..." I stopped her. "Don't do that," I say, and she puts her head down.

"Let's make our way back. We can go for a walk." She nods her head and steers us back to the entrance. We're making our way towards the trail when Avery grabs my hand to stop me.

"I'm sorry, I can't do this," she says when I turn to face her. "You don't want to walk the trail?" I asked her.

"I just can't keep pushing this off till later. We need to talk about this, now," she says. I'm not sure if the tears forming in her eyes are out of frustration or from the wind, but I knew it was time to go. I nodded my head, and we turned back towards the car.

"I'll pick up some drinks on the way back to the cabin," I say when we get in the car. She scoffs and shakes her head. She doesn't say it out loud, but I know what she's thinking. *You only want to grab drinks to hide from what's going on*. If she wanted me to be sober for the conversation, then that's what she would get. Avery walks straight into the room when we arrive, and I follow. She sets her things down on the floor, grabs some sweats and tells me she's going to change. This is going to be a long afternoon. I throw on some leggings and walk over to the sliding doors. I stared out of them, trying to think of what I was going to say when I saw her reflection from the window. I take a deep breath and walk towards the couch. We sat on opposite ends, facing each other and waiting to see who was going to speak first. I'm staring down at my hands, twiddling my fingers when I finally hear her start to speak.

"So, I was thinking, tomorrow on our way home we could call him and ask him to meet us at your house. We could have dinner and talk everything out," she says. *She has to be joking*. "You want us all to have dinner?" I ask. She shrugs and nods her head. I let out a half-suppressed laugh and she scolded me.

"Oh, you're serious?" I ask, trying to keep a straight face.

"Well, what's your plan?" she asks, and I can tell she's getting upset. "I don't know, but I'd rather not be sitting around a table, having dinner, while breaking the news to Ivan. It just sounds… disturbing," I say. *I feel sick just thinking about it*.

"I'll tell him," I hear her say just as I'm saying, "I don't want you to tell him."

"What did you say?" she asks as she sits up straight on the couch. "I don't want you to tell him anything. At least not right now," I say. "You're joking right?" she asks, and I can tell she's angry. *I really should have stopped at the store for drinks.*

"Why?" she asks. I stay quiet.

"Chloe, why?" she asks again, a little louder and I can tell she wants to cry.

"Why not right now?"

"Because!" I exclaim, jumping off the couch.

"Look where we are," I say with my arms out like I'm showing off the cabin for the first time.

"We're five hours from home, in a place where no one knows us. Free to be whoever we want and do whatever we want with no repercussions. Look at the cabin we're staying in. Everything about this weekend screams romance." She looks at me like she can't quite grasp what I'm saying.

"I just think we should give it some time. We can see how things go when we get back home" I say.

"You think being here, in this context, is the reason why I said I love you?" she asks quietly, and I can hear the cracking in her voice. I just stand there looking at her. My heart was racing. She gets up from the couch and goes downstairs.

"Avery," I say, trying to stop her. She puts her hand up and walks away. I let out a breath I didn't realize I was holding and sat back down on the couch. I hear my phone go off and walk over to the bed to grab it.

"Hello?" I say, not even checking to see who it was that was calling me.

"Hi," I hear Lex say on the other end. She sounded so happy. "Do you want to get together for dinner?" she asks. I wasn't in the mood, and I knew Avery wouldn't be either.

"Lex, this is your weekend getaway. Take Sara somewhere nice and enjoy yourselves. It's our last night," I say. "Okay," she says. I was glad she wasn't upset.

"I'll see you in the morning," I say, and we hang up.

"That's not why I said it," I hear Avery say and I turn around. "Chloe, I knew I loved you before we came on this trip. I've spent the last few months trying to hide the way I feel, so I wouldn't lose you. Do you know how hard that's been? To know that I'd fallen head over heels for someone that told me time after time that she doesn't date women? To sit there and hear the story of HER and suddenly understand exactly how she felt?" she says and grabs both of my hands. I could feel the tears starting to form in my eyes. "If going back home, and giving it time is what you want, then I'll wait. Whether it's two weeks, or two months. I'll wait, because knowing that you love me..." Before she can say anything else, I pull her in and kiss her. "We'll figure this out okay, I promise," I say.

I let Avery sleep the next morning while I got up and packed our things. I could hear noise downstairs, but no voices and figured Lex was probably doing the same thing.

"Make coffee and let's enjoy our last morning on the patio," I send to Lex, hoping it's her who's awake and not Sara.

"One step ahead of you. Meet me in five," she replies. I leave out a comfortable outfit for Avery to change into once she gets up and showers, then I head downstairs. Lex is sitting outside with our coffee when I get out there and I join her on the couch.

"Is Avery still asleep?" she asks, and I nod my head. "I packed our things already. She just has to shower and change when she gets up," I say.

"Anyway, how was yesterday?" I ask. She looks over at me and blushes.

"We had so much fun," she says, smiling from ear to ear. We spent the next half hour talking about everything they did yesterday. Lex seemed so excited to be telling me about it and I started to wonder if Avery wanted that. If she wanted to be able to talk to someone about us, tell them all the exciting things we did, tell someone she loved me…but all she'd be able to do is go home and tell Ivan we had a good time. That it was a fun girls rip. The sound of Sara's voice yanks me out of my thoughts and stops Lex from continuing on about their day. "How come you never invite us out here for coffee and laughs?" She asks. Lex and I turn to see her and Avery standing at the back door.

We turn back to each other and smile. Lex gets up from the couch, "I have to finish packing," she pouts and walks back inside. Avery joins me on the couch where we sit quietly for a while. I grabbed her hand under the blanket, and she turned to face me.

"Ready to get back home?" I ask. She rubs her thumbs against my hand.

"Only to prove that nothing is going to change," she says in a teasing voice. I laughed a little and pulled her closer to me. A part of me hoped she was right, but the other part of me knew that no matter what happened, someone was going to get hurt.

"We better start getting our bags ready," I say and Avery nods. We walk inside and Avery has our bags by the front door. I grabbed the keys, and we went back outside.

"How about we meet for breakfast?" Lex yells from the front door as we place our things in the trunk. I look at Avery, waiting for an answer and give Lex a thumbs up. I make one last walk through of the bedroom, making sure nothing was left behind, and just stand in the middle of the room for a second. So much had happened in the four days we were here, and so many things were about to change. I take one last look out of the sliding doors and go back downstairs.

"Ready?" I ask the girls as I reach the bottom step. I watch them all look around as I did and then we leave.

I watch Avery as she looks out the window. It was getting late, and the sun was starting to set. After breakfast, we all decided to head back down to the strip, trying to find any excuse just to say a little longer.

"Ready to be home?" I asked Avery. She looks sleepy, but I can tell she was deep in thought. She smiles slightly and nods her head.

"We have about half an hour before we get there. Are you going to be okay to drive home?" I ask. She sits up in her seat but doesn't look over at me.

"Actually, I'm going to stay with you. I'll head to work from there," she says. I look at her. Half shocked, half concerned. "Ivan called the last time we stopped for gas. I told him I was tired and didn't want to have to drive home. When he finished whining about it, he agreed that it would be safer," she says. I smile at the thought of him whining and Avery laughs. We get back to town and lazily unpack our things from the car.

"I'm going to take a bath," I tell Avery after I finish unpacking my suitcase. I fill the tub with warm water and add as many bubbles as I can. I get in, lean my head back and close my eyes. All I wanted to do was relax. I open my eyes after what felt like a couple of seconds and see Avery sitting across from me. I sit up a little, confused and she laughs.

"Don't worry, it's been like five minutes. At first, I thought you were ignoring me when I asked if I could join you. Then when you didn't move when I got in, I knew you fell asleep," she says.

"So, you've just been staring at me like a weirdo?" I ask jokingly.

"You woke up the minute I sat down," she says. We sit there for a few seconds, just looking at each other, until I see her cheeks turn red and she looks away.

"Can I ask you something?" I ask, breaking the silence. She nods her head.

"Does it bother you that you have to hide this?" I ask.

"Hide what?" she asks.

"Us. Does it bother you that we had an incredible weekend, and you don't have anyone to talk to about it?" I ask. Has that ever crossed her mind? I can tell that she hasn't put much thought into it by the way she was looking at me.

"I was just wondering. Lex and I were sitting outside this morning, and she could not stop talking about the day her and Sara had. I could tell how excited she was, and it just got me thinking, like, Avery doesn't have that. She doesn't get to go home and tell someone about the fun weekend she had and who she had it with," I say.

"Yeah…" she says. *I knew it would upset her, but I wanted to know.*

"Let's finish up in here and go lay down. We don't want to be tired tomorrow," she says. I get into bed before she does. Ivan called her as soon as she got out of the bath, and she got dressed and went into the kitchen to talk to him. I was dozing off when I felt her get into bed. She tossed and turned and sighed until I finally opened my eyes.

"Do you want to talk about it?" I ask sleepily, and without hesitation, she responds.

"Does it not bother you?" she asks. I was more asleep than awake, but I knew what she was asking me. I rolled over to face her.

"It bothers me that it bothers you," I say. "But personally, no. It doesn't bother me."

"Why are you like this?" she asks, now sitting up.

"Ivan's always talked about how you hold everything in, but are you going to be like that with me too?"

"Ivan?" I ask, leaning up slightly.

"Oh, Chloe. Come on," she says, and I can tell she's getting frustrated. I sat up and leaned towards her.

"I'll talk to you," I say and kiss her shoulder. "I promise," and kiss her cheek. "But not right now," I pull her back down on the bed and she stares at me. "Right now, I want to go to sleep," I say and throw the covers over her head. She laughs and I turn back around, trying to get comfortable. I feel her wrap her arm around me and even though deep down I know it's wrong, everything about it feels right. I can't help but think of the mess that's yet to come.

PART THREE

The Deception

Avery's gone by the time my alarm goes off in the morning. A part of me was sad to be back, but the other part of me was ready to get back to reality. I get up to start the coffee pot and start getting ready for work. I think about the past few days as I'm getting ready and thinking about what Andres said. *Would Ivan really understand*? Maybe the space would make Avery change her mind. Maybe she was just so lost in the moment while we were away that she felt like that. *Would it bother me if that were true? I said I loved her too. If in a few days, or weeks or even a month from now, if she changed her mind...would it affect me*? I heard the coffee pot go off and headed to the room to grab my clothes. My phone buzzes on the nightstand as I'm walking out, but I don't check it. I'm already running late. Once I'm dressed, I pour my coffee, grab my things and I'm out the door. After settling in and responding to what felt like a million emails, I decided to check my phone. There were a few social media notifications, a text from Lex from last night letting me know they made it home and a message from Avery. *That's from this morning.*

"Good morning, you looked so comfortable this morning, I didn't want to wake you up. I just wanted to let you know I made it home. Thank you for such an amazing weekend, I already can't wait to go back. I hope you have a great day. I love you, Chloe." I feel a dull ache in my chest.

"Glad you made it back safely. I love you," I responded and put my phone away in my desk. After a few hours of non-stop work, I got up and stretched my legs and noticed the sun was beginning to set. I close everything out, grab my things and leave for the day. I stopped to grab dinner, knowing I didn't have any groceries and headed home. After dinner, I checked my phone hoping to find nothing. Avery called around three and again right before six. There were a few messages from her as well.

"Sorry, you're probably busy. I just wanted to say hi." "Chloe, are you ignoring me?"

"I'll take that as a yes. Ivan will be home soon. I'll just talk to you tomorrow, or whenever." I decided not to respond. I know Ivan goes to bed earlier than she does, so I wait awhile, busying myself with things around the house. It was a little after nine and I figured now would be a good time to call. She picks up on the first ring.

"Hi," she says calmly.

"Hi, Avery," I say. I can sense her smiling on the other end. "Sorry I took forever to reply. I got to work this morning and just lost track of time. I got home around seven," I say.

"Oh, wow. I'm sorry. I thought..." she pauses.

"I know, but I promised you, remember? And not just so you would go to sleep," I say, and she laughs. "I'm sorry," she says again. "Anyway, I better let you. Good night, Avery," I say.

"Good night love," she says cautiously and after a couple of seconds, she hangs up.

The rest of the week seemed to fly by. I talked to Avery before, during and after work each day. It was going to take some getting used to, but I enjoyed it. On Friday evening, just as I was getting settled in after work, my phone began to ring.

"Ivan" I read on the screen, and suddenly my heart began to race. I answer the phone as calmly as possible.

"Hey, Ivan," I say.

"Chloe," he says in a stern voice and my heart drops. *He knows.* "I can't believe you were gone all weekend and haven't called me today to say that you're on your way." I laugh and let out a sigh of relief. "What?" I say.

"Pack your bags and get on the road," he says, still trying to keep the stern voice going, but I can tell he wants to laugh too.

"Ivan, I'm tired. I was going to wait till Sunday. You know, to give you and Avery the weekend to yourselves," I say.

"Don't worry, I've had her alone all week," he says, and I can hear Avery say his name in the background. She sounded embarrassed. "Ouch. What was that for?" I hear him from a distance while laughing. "Seriously, Chloe. Pack your bags and get your ass over here. It's not even that late yet. You can relax when you get here," he says. I sigh. "Alright. I'll see you in a little while," I say.

"Hell yeah," he exclaims. I smile and hang up the phone. *Well, there goes my whole plan of giving Avery and I some space. Would it be any different from any other weekend I've spent there? Other than the fact that I was now in love with her? I need to be sure to give her the same minimal attention that I had before and hope she doesn't get offended by it.*

"Everything will be fine," I repeat to myself as I begin to pack my things. Half an hour later I was on the road. I sent Ivan a message, letting him know I was just a few minutes away and he let me know he would be in the backyard. Skipping dinner and going straight to bed sounded so good, but there was no way in hell Ivan was going to let that happen. I missed him, and suddenly I was sad at the thought of losing him. I grabbed my bag out of the car and headed inside. I walk straight into the guest bedroom to put down my things before I go to the back to see Ivan. I'm making my way out of the room when Avery runs in, wraps me in her arms and kisses me.

"Hi," I say, trying to catch my breath. She smiles at me and kisses me one more time before she lets me go. "I've been waiting to do that since I left your house the other morning. I missed you," she says. I smile at her. My heart was still racing.

"I have to go say hi to Ivan," I say shyly and make my way out of the room. *Why was I so nervous, and why was it so hot in here*? I practically ran out the back door and almost tackled Ivan off the porch steps.

"Hug me back!" I say laughing.

"Don't make it weird," he says sarcastically. I stepped back and looked at him.

"Need I remind you that about two hours ago you were damn near begging for me to come over," I say jokingly.

"Yeah right," he says embarrassed.

"And yesterday too," Avery says from the back door. Ivan and I both turned to look at her.

"She's lying," he says, looking back at me and laughing.

"You know what, I actually don't like that the two of you are friends," he says.

"Too bad," Avery and I both say at the same time. Ivan shakes his head, and we laugh.

"It's cold. Go inside. The food is almost done," he says. Avery and I headed into the kitchen, and I took a seat at the table.

"You want a glass of wine?" Avery asks.

"Only if you're having one," I say. She pours two glasses and walks over to me, placing mine on the table, but not taking a seat. She stands directly in front of me, lifting my head with her hand to meet her gaze.

"He's going to see us," I say, looking towards the back door. "Maybe it's time," she says quietly.

"Avery," I say, and she cuts me off, taking my head in her hand again to face her.

"Do you love me?" she asks. I nod my head. She stares at me for what feels like forever and then drops her hand.

"Then we'll wait," she says and takes a seat next to me. I smile at her and take a sip of my wine. *What the hell was that*? Ivan walks in a few minutes later with our plates. He made hibachi on the black top, and it smelled so good.

"Babe, will you grab me a beer?" he asks Avery as he sets our plates down. He watches her as she rounds the table and just when she's far enough, he steals her spot next to me and places her plate across from us. I watch him the whole time, trying not to laugh and when she turns back around, we lose it. She rolls her eyes at us and slides the bottle across the table.

"Don't be mad babe. You got to be with her all weekend. Let me have my best friend for a night," he says and the dull ache in my heart returns. We enjoyed our dinner as I told Ivan all about our trip. He's heard Avery's versions, of course, but he wanted to hear mine.

"I want to go one weekend. I've always loved hearing about it when you go," Ivan says.

"The two of you should make a trip," I say, and I can feel Avery look at me, but I don't return her gaze.

"Maybe one of these weekends," he says, not noticing the change in Avery's expression. He then tells me about all the stuff he did while we were gone. Which was his way of silently asking us to never leave him again. Avery and I shared side glances at each other, trying to keep our composure, and we let him finish. Ivan takes our plates to the sink when we're done and tops us all off with our final glass of wine.

"Well, I'm going to shower if you don't mind," I said to Ivan as I finished my glass. Ivan nods his head and I go into the bedroom to grab my things. I stand in the shower, letting the warm water hit my shoulders and feel myself begin to relax. I hadn't realized how tense I had been, or how difficult this would be. Avery sure wasn't making it any easier. If it were anyone else, I'd say to leave him, but it was Ivan. Telling him means hurting him. Not only does he lose his girlfriend, but he loses his best friend too. Not telling him means losing her and in the end still losing him, because being around them would be too hard. I finish my shower and take my things back to the room. I can hear the T.V. on in the living room. They must be watching a movie. Just before walking in, I see Ivan and Avery cuddled on the couch. I watch them for a second before entering.

"Hey, I'm going to go to bed already," I say, catching them both off guard.

"No. Come watch T.V. with us," Avery says, attempting to make room.

"I'm tired. Plus, the shower and the wine didn't help," I say. Ivan smiles at me.

"Get some rest. We'll see you in the morning," he says. I close the bedroom door behind me and lay down. Just as I was starting to fall asleep, I felt my phone buzz next to me.

"Will you wait up for me?" I read on the screen, but I don't reply. I wanted her here, next to me, but I didn't want to make it obvious. They look so comfortable with each other, how's was Avery so willing to just give that up? I should just go to sleep.

It's quiet when I wake up the next morning. I quietly sneak out of the room to wash up, then go into the kitchen to make some coffee. *They must of went to bed late*. When the coffee was done, I make myself a cup, grab a blanket from the couch and go out to the back porch. The sun was out, so it wasn't too cold, but I wrapped myself up and sat anyway. There was a silence, and for the first time in weeks, my mind was not racing with thoughts of what if's. A few moments pass and I hear the back door open. I sit there, not turning to see who it is.

"I knew you'd be out here," Ivan says as he sits next to me. I turn to face him and smile.

"Late night?" I asked, nudging him slightly, knowing very well I didn't want to know the answer. He laughs.

"No. I fell asleep on the couch," he pauses.

"And Avery left me there." I laugh as he takes a sip of his coffee. "How's everything been? It's been a while since we've had one of our talks," he says. I thought about the question I asked Avery the other night. I guess in a way it did bother me, because I couldn't talk to Ivan about us.

"It's been good," I say, trying to sound convincing.

"Plus, I love being able to run away on the weekends." He smiles at me.

"You look happy. I guess getting them out of your life has been good for you," he says. He was talking about HER and Alex. *That feels like a whole lifetime ago*.

"I never get invited to backyard talks," we hear Avery say from the back door and we laugh.

"Well, that's my cue," he says. He squeezes my leg and gets up to give Avery his seat.

"Guess I'll go make breakfast," he says sarcastically and walks inside. Avery scoots in next to me as I lift the blanket and puts her hand in mine. I don't pull away from her this time, instead I move closer.

"Not afraid anymore?" she asks.

"It's cold. He won't think anything of it," I say. She scoots in closer.

"How did you sleep last night? I tried to text you because he was falling asleep," she says.

"I know, I saw it this morning. I was so tired. I fell asleep as soon as I laid down," I said. She looks over at me.

"Can I sleep with you tonight?" she asks. I nod my head without looking over at her. *I'm slowly starting to realize it's easier not to fight with her. Especially after yesterday.*

"Chloe?" she says. There was a change in her tone. "I'm sorry about what Ivan said on the phone yesterday." I look at her confused, trying to think back to our conversation.

"The whole having me alone," she says mockingly.

"I'm sorry he said that and I'm sorry you saw us cuddled on the couch last night. Honestly, I didn't even sleep. I was worried..." I put my hand up and shook my head, attempting to cut her off.

"No," I say, still shaking my head. "I do not care to hear about what happened or didn't happen," I say.

"But we..." I cut her off again.

"Avery, stop," I say. She looks at me. Half embarrassed, half upset. "It doesn't bother me. I was the one that decided you should stay with him, knowing that I would still have to see the two of you together. Just spare me the details, okay?" She looked surprised. She stayed quiet for a minute.

"You're seeing someone else," she says. It sounded like more of a statement than a question.

"What?" I say, trying to contain my laughter.

"That's why you don't want me to leave him, because you're seeing someone else," she says.

"Avery, I'm..." She gets up from her seat.

"We should go inside," she says as she walks away. I just sat there, lost. *She has every right to think that. She knows me. She knows the relationships I have with women, and she knows how they work. But the truth was, the only reason I didn't want her to leave Ivan is because I watts ready to lose him. So, I had to put up with seeing them together.* "Chloe," I hear Ivan say and nearly fall out of my seat. I stood quickly and turned to face him. The look on his face causes immediate laughter and he joins me.

"You scared the hell out of me," I say, swatting his arm as I walked past him.

"I was just trying to let you know breakfast was ready," he says, following me inside. Avery was not at the table when we entered the kitchen, and I only noticed two plates.

"Avery went to take a shower," Ivan says as he takes his seat. I don't say anything as I sit down. *She's upset*.

"I have to go out to the shop after we finish up here," he says. I look over at him. "I thought you were off this weekend?" I ask.

"We got a new guy," he says, annoyed.

"I have to go in and help him out for a bit, but hey. There's this nice restaurant/bar place that just opened. I thought we could all go." "Sounds perfect," I say. We finish our food, and he goes into their room to get ready for work. I pick up our plates from the table and take them over to the sink. I looked around the kitchen for a second and decided to clean. Even though Ivan hates it when I do. I can hear him and Avery talking in the room. She sounds upset about him going to work.

Probably even more so since she was upset with me. I finish loading the dishwasher and go back into the room to lay down.

There's a knock at the door. "Chloe," I hear Avery say from the other side. I opened my eyes, not realizing I had fallen asleep. I hear the door crack open slowly and turn around. She was walking in quietly, not noticing I was awake.

"Hi," I say in a sleepy voice, and she freezes.

"Sorry, I didn't want to wake you," she says, not looking up at me. She stands at the edge of the bed. I sat up, waiting for her to say something.

"Are you just going to stand there?" I asked her. She looks up at me and I stretch out my hand.

"Come here," I say, and she crawls on the bed towards me. She lays her head on my chest and wraps her arms around me. I kiss the top of her head and run my fingers through her hair.

"I think I overreacted," she says in a quiet, muffled voice. I laugh.

"You think?" I say and she lifts her head to look at me. She frowns and moves to sit across from me.

"Are you going to let me explain, or just sit there and make fun of me?" she asks, and I laugh again. She throws her legs over the side of the bed, and I reach forward to grab her arm.

"Wait," I say, trying to catch my breath.

"Ok, I'm sorry. I'm done now," I say as she glares at me. She repositions herself on the bed.

"I'm sorry too," she says.

"You don't have to be," I say, moving closer to hold her hand. "Avery, you have every right to question this."

"What?" she asks, confused.

"You know me. You know how I do things. Not to sound cliche or anything, but this *is* different. I've never loved any of the women I've ever been with," I say.

"If this is so different, then why are you making me wait? Why can't we just be together?" she asks.

"Because of Ivan. He's my best friend Avery. It would break him," I say. She takes a deep breath and grabs both of my hands.

"Look. I know you're trying to protect him, but sometimes you have to think about yourself. What about what you want? Don't get me wrong, I love Ivan, and I hate that this will hurt him. But I'm in love with you Chloe," she says. I stared down at my hands, interlocked with hers. She removes one of her hands and tilts my head up.

"We're still going to wait, aren't we?" she asks, and I nod my head. She smiles at me.

"You have a beautiful heart, Chloe. That's part of the reason why I fell in love with you," she says, leaning towards me.

"What's the other reason?" I ask, teasingly. She raises an eyebrow. "Let me show you."

As the weeks went by, my love for Avery continued to grow. Ivan's job started to get busier, which required more of his time. He started working six days a week and on Sunday's all he wanted to do was rest. That alone allowed Avery and I to spend more time together without seeming suspicious. Christmas was next week and of course,

Ivan had to work. Avery was going to spend the holiday with her family, and we agreed to end the night together. Two days before I met up with Lex and Sara for lunch. We hadn't seen each other since the trip, so it was good to be able to catch up with them.

"How's Avery?" Lex asks and I smile. "That good, huh?"

"She's great," I say, still with the same cheesy smile on my face. "She's spending Christmas with her family, but we'll end it together." "Happy looks good on you," Sara says.

"So, we had drinks with everyone the other night," Lex says and Sara glances over at her with one of those 'what are you doing?' looks.

"I was showing the girls pics from our trip, and they saw one of you and Avery."

"Okay..." I say, waiting for her to continue.

"She saw the picture," Lex says, staring down at her plate.

"I told HER the two of you were together." I laugh. Sara and Lex look at each other confused.

"I bet she was pissed," I say, still laughing. Lex smiles nervously.

"I'm sorry Chloe," Lex says.

"For what? I mean, it's none of her business, but I don't care that she knows," I say. Lex stays quiet for a second.

"She was pretty pissed," she says, and we all laugh. I spent the next day cleaning and decorating. I knew we weren't actually spending Christmas together, but I wanted it to be perfect. I bought her a necklace, even though we promised each other nothing too expensive, and stuck a note in the box.

"It's time." Avery had been very patient, and just like she said, her feelings did not change. Did I still feel bad? Yes, of course, but I wanted to be with her, more than anything. I woke the next morning to a message from Ivan and one from Avery. As I was reading the message from Ivan, I heard a knock at the door. *That couldn't be Avery. Surely, she would have called.* I put my phone down and got out of bed. No one was there. I looked down and found a coffee and a bag, which I assumed was food. I took it into the kitchen and found a note in the bag.

"Merry Christmas." My phone rang and I ran to my room to get it.

"Hi," I say.

"Merry Christmas love," Avery says on the other end. "Eat your breakfast."

"Oh my gosh, it was you," I say, and she starts laughing.

"I knew if I saw you, I wouldn't want to leave, so I just dropped it off," she says.

"That's not fair," I say.

"I know. I'll see you tonight. I love you," she says and hangs up. I go back to read the message from Ivan.

"Merry Christmas, Chloe. I hope you get everything you wished for." The dull ache returns.

"Merry Christmas. I wish you could be here. I'll see you in a few days," I send back and head into the kitsch to eat. I spent the rest of the day lounging around, waiting for Avery. It was a little after five when she texted that she was on her way. I had just finished setting the table when she walked in.

"Ooh, it smells good in here," she says as she walks into the kitchen.

"Come sit down," I say and fix our plates. We talk about how Christmas went with her family as we eat. I was glad she got to see them, between Ivan and I, she really had not been around them much.

"That was so good. Thank you," she said as she grabbed our plates from the table. I go to my room to grab her present and go back to the table.

"Chloe, I thought we agreed that we weren't getting anything expensive," she says when I hand her the box.

"Will you just open it," I say. She opens the gift and I watch as her eyes begin to water.

"Does this mean…?" she asks as her voice cracks. "We can finally…" she attempts to say again. I reached to grab her hand and pulled her into my arms. She hugs me tightly.

"When?" she asks.

"At the beginning of the year," I say. She hugged me again. "Thank you for waiting," I say.

"I love you, Avery."

Ivan was off the weekend after Christmas, and I told Avery I wanted to spend one more weekend with him.

"He's going to hate me. You know that, right?" I tell her over the phone the night before I go over.

"And then after that, we're good right?" She asks.

"Yes," I say, noticing she disregarded that whole statement. "Good. Even if you said no, I was going to tell him anyway," she says laughing.

"Avery, that's not funny," I say.

"What's not funny is you making me wait two damn months. Do you know how hard it is to pretend you love someone day in and day out?" she says. I process what she said for a second.

"I thought you still loved Ivan?" I ask.

"I have love for him, don't get me wrong. But I'm in love with you, and not just for the past two months," she says.

"Hey babe," I hear Ivan say in the background. I hear what sounds like a kiss and almost hang up.

"Is it Chloe?" I heard him ask.

"Yeah," she says, and puts me on speaker.

"Chloe!" I hear him yell. "What time are you coming tomorrow?"

"Probably sometime after lunch," I say. "

Wow, you're still off too?" he asks.

"I hate you." Avery and I laughed.

"Well since you'll be here early, and I'm the only one that has to work, then the two of you can make me dinner," he says.

"Deal," I say.

"I better go," Avery says, and we hang up. I sit on my bed, reminiscing on all the years I had been friends with Ivan. I could feel the warm tears begin to roll down my face. *Is it worth it? Is the love I have for Avery really worth losing Ivan for? Who would we turn to when something goes wrong? Who would he turn to when he finds out? He would be alone. He'd suffer not only one, but two heartbreaks.* My heart hurts as I continue to question everything. I go into the bathroom to wash my face and go back into my room to pack. I thought about texting Avery to tell her I wanted to spend one whole day with Ivan, but I didn't. *You have to think about yourself sometimes*, I hear her say in my head. Spending the whole day with Ivan could easily change my mind. Not out of lack of love for Avery, but for the love I have for Ivan. I went to bed early that night, though I didn't sleep much. I feel an emptiness in my heart when I wake up the next morning but get up and shower anyway. Avery calls as I'm getting my things ready. She was full of energy this morning and I tried to sound excited to be going. I drove in silence, flashbacks of Ivan going through my mind. I was torturing myself. I wanted a drink but most of all, I wanted all of this to be over. I pulled into the driveway and checked myself in the mirror before I got off. My eyes were still a little swollen. I hope she doesn't notice. She greets me at the door, and I try my best not to look at her. She hugs me and I fight back the tears forming in my eyes.

"How was your drive?" she asks as she takes my bags to the room

"It felt like forever," I say, following behind her.

"Why don't we spend the day laying on the couch watching movies?" Well at least until we have to get up and cook," she says, rolling her eyes.

"That sounds perfect," I say. We recline back on the couch as Avery scrolls, trying to find a movie and she reaches over and grabs my hand.

"Are you okay? You look tired," she says.

"Yeah. I didn't sleep very well last night," I say. She pulls me into her arms.

"Take a nap. I'll wake you up in a couple of hours," she says. I rest my head on her shoulder and quickly fall asleep.

"How could you do this to me?" Ivan asks, standing right in front of me. He had tears in his eyes, but he didn't look sad. He was angry. "Chloe, why? Why her? You could have anyone you want, and you chose her?" I couldn't speak. I opened my mouth, but no words came out.

"I love her!" he shouts.

"And I loved you. I will never forgive you for this. I never want to see you again."

"Chloe. Chloe, wake up. Please," I hear Avery saying. She was holding my head in her hands, and I jolted up. My heart was racing, I kept trying to catch my breath.

"I think you were having a bad dream," she says, moving my hair out of my face. I look around, trying to steady myself and trying to separate dream from reality. I sit back on the couch and take a deep breath. Avery looked terrified.

"I'm sorry," I say. She shakes her head.

"You don't have to apologize Chloe." I pulled her into my arms and just held her for a minute. She let go of me, taking my hands in hers. "Are you okay?" she asks. I nod my head.

"I'm sweaty," I say, and she laughs.

"What time is it?" "We have about two hours before Ivan comes home," she says.

"I'm going to take a quick shower, then we can start dinner," I say and walk away.

"Damn!" I hear Ivan say as he walks through the door. "It smells good in here." I'm setting the table when he walks into the kitchen. He walks up to Avery, grabs her by the waist and goes in for a kiss. She moves her head slightly to the left, so he kisses her cheek. I see him pull back and look at her and she shakes her head.

"We made you steak and shrimp," I say, not looking up at them. "I knew you loved me. Let me go change," he says. Avery follows him out of the kitchen, and I make our plates. I can hear them whispering as I grab Ivan a beer from the fridge. I knew she was going to tell him about what happened.

"Just don't bring it up," I hear her say as they walk out of the room. I watched Ivan cut into his steak and take a bite. His eyes roll back in appreciation, and he looks at me and smiles. "I know you made this," he says. Avery gives him a questioning look and Ivan and I laugh.

"Sorry babe, but Chloe is the only one that can cook a steak almost as good as I can. I still love your cooking though," he says. "Thanks for the backhanded compliment," I say. She smiles at me, and we continue eating. Avery picks up our plates when we're done and Ivan nods his head toward the living room, signaling us to leave the kitchen. I look at Avery as I'm walking away, but she doesn't return my gaze. We sit on the couch and before he gets a word out, I speak.

"Don't make this more than what it is, Ivan. It was just a bad dream," I say. I can tell I caught him off guard by the expression on his face.

"I know she told you." He keeps his eyes on me but doesn't say anything.

"Ivan…I," I freeze as my voice becomes hoarse. I wanted so badly to tell him, to just get it over with. But I didn't have the heart to do it. Instead, I sat up and cleared my throat.

"I'm sorry, if I worried you," I say. He reaches for my hand and gives me a kind smile.

"Promise you're okay?" He asks. I nod my head.

"Now, if you don't mind. I'm going to the room. I've had a long day," I say as I get up from the couch. I watch him laugh and shake his head and then I leave the room. I lay on the bed for a while but didn't fall asleep. There's a knock at the door and I sit up as I watch Avery walk in.

"Sorry, were you asleep?" she asks.

"Coming to check up on me?" I asked, annoyed. I was mad that she told Ivan about what happened. It wasn't a big deal. I knew she was worried, but it still made me upset.

"Chloe, I'm sorry," she says and walks towards the bed. I watch as she stands there, and I lift the covers so she can sit down.

"Are you mad at me?" she asks, and I can hear the nervousness in her voice.

"No. I just don't know why you had to tell him," I say.

"I really am sorry Chloe. After your shower you just stayed quiet and I wasn't sure what to do," she says. Without thinking I look over at her and say "And what are you going to do when you leave him? Call him and ask for advice?" I was just as shocked as she was at the words that had just come out of my mouth. She moves to get off the bed. "Avery, wait," I say. She walks to the door and as she reaches for the knob, she stops and turns around.

"I'm sorry I didn't handle it in a way that is acceptable to you, but I'm not sorry for being worried about you," she snaps at me. I get out of bed and walk towards her.

"Avery, I'm sorry. Stay with me, please. At least until I fall asleep," I say.

"Only if you tell me what happened," she says. I took her hand and led her back to the bed. I sit down on the edge so that I'm facing her and start with everything that happened yesterday up until the dream.

"I didn't realize you were taking this so hard," she says, looking down at her hands.

"It just hit me. I mean, I've thought about it, of course. It's never bothered me this bad though," I say.

"It's because it's the last weekend. Unless..." she pauses. I lift her head, so she'll look at me.

"I'm not backing out Avery," I say. She lets out a small cry, which I assume was of relief and hugs me. I held her tightly and moved to lay down so that I could sleep.

Ivan's already up when I wake the next morning. I walk down the hall and lean on the doorway of the living room. He looks over at me and I smile.

"There's coffee in the kitchen," he says, and I make myself a cup. I join him on the couch, and he turns down the T.V. a little.

"Is Avery still asleep?" he asks. I nod my head and take a sip of my coffee.

"Can I ask you something?" I freeze. I turn to look at him. "Anything," I say.

"Has Avery mentioned anything to you?" he asks. I look at him confused.

"Like about us? She's been so distant lately. I know I've been working a lot. I was just wondering if she's said anything." I shake my head.

"No. She hasn't said anything," I say. "I took the next few days off. I want to take her out," he says. *She's supposed to leave him at the beginning of the year.*

"Where are you thinking about going?" I ask, trying to stay in the conversation. He smiles at me. *Of course. He wants to take her to the cabins.*

"So, what do you think?" he asks. "I think she'll love it," I say. He sits back and smiles.

"Yeah, I think she will too," he says. "My phone buzzed, and I saw Avery's name on the screen.

"Come back and lay down with me." I read and set my phone back down. A million thoughts race through my mind. *Should I tell her? Will she be mad if I don't? What if she doesn't want to go? What if she goes and she changes her mind*? I got up and walked back to the room.

"Well, it took you long enough," Avery says when I walk back into the room. I look at her and she sits up.

"What happened?" she asks. I get in bed and sit next to her.

"I woke up way too early," I say and laugh.

"Dammit, Chloe. You scared me," she exclaims. "Shh. Don't be loud. Ivan will make us get up," I say, and we try our best to hold in our laughter. I lay my head on her lap as she caresses my arm.

"So, what really happened?" she asks. I turned over to look up at her. "When are you going to accept the fact that I know you?" I sit up and move to sit across from her.

"He wants to take you on a trip. He took the next few days off, it's supposed to be a surprise," I say. She laughs and I watch her whole demeanor change.

"So, you just weren't going to tell me?" she asks. "Avery…" I say as she cuts me off.

"No. You really weren't going to say anything? You were just going to leave tomorrow and let him surprise me? I'm not going Chloe," she says as she gets off the bed. She was upset and she had every right to be.

"I didn't want to be the reason you didn't go. I mean, it's a trip with Ivan. I thought I'd give you one last chance to see if this is what you really want. Plus, he wants to take you to the cabins..." I say and she cuts me off again.

"The cabins?" she asks.

"Avery, please keep your voice down," I say. She shakes her head and looks away from me.

"Let me guess, you want me to go on the trip as another way to prove that it's you I want to be with? Chloe, I love you, but if you don't stop feeling guilty it's going to ruin us," she says. There's a knock at the door. Avery looks over at me and walks out of the room. Hot tears begin to build as she leaves. I wanted to scream. I wanted to pack my things and leave. I wanted to storm out of the room and tell Ivan everything while Avery packed her things to leave with me. But I was too much of a coward. So instead, I turned back towards the bed and quietly cried myself to sleep.

I hear the front door close as I'm getting out of the shower. *They must have gone out.* I wrap myself in a towel and go back into the room. Avery's sitting on the bed when I walk in.

"I thought you left," I say, pulling my clothes out of my bag. "Ivan went to run a few errands…" she pauses, "for the trip." I stop what I'm doing and look up at her.

"He asked me when I left the room earlier," she says as she gets off the bed and walks towards me.

"Don't worry baby," she says in a playful voice as she wraps her arms around me.

"I acted like I was excited when I said yes." I pull away from her and she drops her hands.

"What? This is what you wanted isn't it?" Her tone changed quickly. *Why is she acting like this*? I change into my clothes and start putting my things into my bag.

"What are you doing?" she asks. I could still hear the anger in her voice.

"I'm not doing this with you. I'm going home," I say as I continue packing.

"What happened to spending your last weekend with Ivan? Or does that suddenly not matter anymore?" she asks. I can feel my eyes begin to water again and I try my hardest not to look up at her.

"What's wrong Chloe? Suddenly you have nothing to say?" she asks. She's trying to get a rise out of me because she's angry, but I don't give her the satisfaction.

"Afraid I'm going to fall back in love with him?" she asks. I look up at her this time, tears rolling down my face. I watch her expression change instantly. "Chloe, I.." she says quietly.

"I hope you have a great time," I say as I grab my things and leave the room. She reaches for my hand as I walk past her.

"Don't," I say, moving away from her.

"Chloe, I didn't…" I hear her say from behind me, but I'm out the door before she can finish. I throw my bag in the front seat and leave before she can try to come out and stop me. Tears were still rolling down my face as I was driving, and my chest felt heavy. We had never fought like this before, and she had never talked to me that way. I hear my phone go off and without looking at the screen, I silence it and throw it in my bag. I drove in silence all the way home and an hour later I was curled up in my bed as her words played on repeat in my head. *What's wrong Chloe? Afraid I'm going to fall back in love with him? Had I finally pushed her past her limit? I've pulled her in and pushed her away for so long, maybe she's finally tired of it.* I pull my phone out of my bag and check my messages. There were calls from Avery every other minute after I left and then they stopped. That must have been when Ivan got home. There was a text from him.

"Avery said there was an emergency and you had to leave? I hope everything is okay. Be safe Chloe." I didn't respond back. I leave my phone on the bed and go into the kitchen to grab something to eat. All I had this morning was coffee and it was already after five. After staring at the fridge for a few minutes I decided I'd go get takeout. I was not in the mood to cook. I drive around town, passing restaurants. Nothing sounded good. I found myself parked in front of the liquor store about fifteen minutes later. There's that voice in my head again. *Why do you always have to drink when something is wrong*?

"Oh, fuck off Avery," I say out loud.

"That's just who I am." I get out of the car and walk inside. *Okay. Whiskey or tequila? Definitely whiskey.* I grab a bottle and take it up to the counter.

"Chloe… hey," I hear someone say as I walk out of the store. I don't look up to see who it is. I just kept walking towards my car. When I get home, I grab a small glass and fill it with ice. I contemplate whether I should mix it or drink it straight. I pace the kitchen back and forth, contemplating whether or not I should call Avery. I hear a knock at the door that brings me out of the daze I had been in.

"Alex?" I say when I open the door. "Hey. I saw you leaving the liquor store. I called out your name, you looked kind of distraught. I just thought I'd come by and check on you," he says. He looked worried. "I'm fine," I say, shutting the door.

"Chloe are you sure?" he asks, stepping backwards. "Just leave."

I have to see her. I have to tell her that I'm sorry. I drive aimlessly around the city. Okay. Ivan's lowkey, he doesn't like crowds. I think of small restaurants, stores, and different places on the strip. I knew this city in and out. It was only a matter of time before I found her.

"The lake," I say out loud. *He loved it when I talked about the lake. I'm sure she told him about it too*. I drive quickly down the highway, swerving in and out of traffic. They had to be there. There's no way I would find them if they stayed in. I pulled into the lake half an hour later. I drive slowly by the parked cars, trying to spot his.

"There it is," I say. "They're here." I try to find parking while I think about where they could be. I'm standing next to my car, looking around, and right as I'm about to take a step, I hear his voice behind me. "Chloe?" I turn around.

"What are you doing here?" he asks. I keep my eyes on Avery, never looking at Ivan.

"Never mind that. I have big news!" he exclaims. My eyes still never leaving Avery's.

"I asked Avery to marry me," he says as he lifts her hand.

"She said yes!" I open my eyes and try to catch my breath. My heart was racing, and my head was pounding. I sit up on the couch and lean my head back, regretting every drink. Once I catch my breath, I walk into the kitchen to grab a glass of water. I notice my phone on the counter and pick it up, bypassing every notification and open Avery's messages. I don't read any of them, I just start typing.

"Avery, please don't go." My phone dies the minute I hit send. I drop my head and take a deep breath. Once I find my charger, I plug my phone in and go into the bathroom to shower. I was so hungover, and though I didn't have much of an appetite, I knew I needed to eat. But most of all, I needed Avery here with me. I showered longer than I intended too. Trying to wash the guilt off. I threw on a sweater and some shorts then went into my room to check my phone. Avery had replied. "Chloe, I'm sorry. We left this morning. We're almost there. I need you to know that I love you, so much! I promise to go straight to you when I get back. And just so you know, I don't plan on leaving once I'm there. I'll see you in two days." A huge sense of relief runs through my body as I read her message. I feel my shoulders begin to relax and I drop down onto my bed. I know there was a lot we would have to discuss, but right now, all I was thinking about was her coming home, to me, and I drifted off to sleep.

That nap was very much needed. My stomach began to growl as I rolled out of bed. I grab my phone to order takeout and walk into the living room to clean. There wasn't a mess, but I needed to put up the bottle and pick up the pillows. As I'm cleaning up, I notice my front door was slightly cracked open. *Did it stay like that all night*?

"Oh my gosh, Alex," I say out loud. I completely forgot he showed up last night. I laugh to myself. *I was a wreck, and he saw me.* I finish picking up and grab my keys so I can go. I open the front door and Alex is standing on the porch with one of his arms up as if he was just about to knock.

"Wow. Twice in twenty-four hours. Lucky me," I say, shutting the door and walking past him.

"I just wanted to check on you. You were a mess yesterday. Is everything ok? You look like you haven't slept in days," he says. I laugh.

"Geez, thanks Alex," I say. He stands there with the same concerned look on his face. I roll my eyes at him.

"I'm fine. Not that it's any of your business." He nods his head. "Okay then," he says, and I watch him as he walks off. I sat on my couch and ate my dinner as I flipped through the channels on the T.V. I flip till I find some sort of rom-com and finish my food. I was never one to go all day without eating, even if I was upset, and I never drank on an empty stomach. Yesterday was rough, but I was happy Avery would be home in a couple of days. I get up to throw away my plate and grab the small blanket off the other couch. I had been so tense with everything that had been going on, I was glad to be home, doing absolutely nothing. At some point, I dozed off, and woke up to the sounds of my phone ringing. I got up and walked to the kitchen, trying to find my phone. *Andres? Why would he be calling me right now?*

"Hello," I say. "Hi, Chloe," he sounds conflicted.

"Hi," I say back. *Andres was never one to call out of the blue. In fact, the only time we talked was when I was in the city.*

"What are you up to?" he asks. "I was just lying on the couch watching T.V.," I say.

"Ooh, a nice quiet night in," he says. *Okay, something's wrong.* I let out a small laugh.

"Andres, not that I don't mind the small talk, but what's up?" I ask. He's quiet for a minute.

"She's here," he says finally.

"The woman that you were with. I'm guessing you never got around to telling the boyfriend?" Now I was the one who was quiet. I was trying to wrap my head around the thought of them being there. I had never mentioned the restaurant to Ivan. It had to have been Avery. "Chloe, I need to tell you something," he says, and I feel a lump develop in my throat.

"After dinner, he ordered a bottle of wine. We're short staffed tonight, so I brought it down from the bar. I didn't recognize her until after I poured her glass."

"Okay…" I said nervously. "He said something as I was walking away…" he pauses for a second. I was becoming impatient. The anticipation was killing me.

"What did he say Andres?" I ask, practically yelling.

"I want to spend the rest of my life with you Avery." I freeze and feel my whole-body tense up. My phone fell out of my hand. I hear the faint sound of his voice coming from my phone. "Chloe! Chloe, are you there? What happened?"

Emptiness. Confusion. Betrayal. Sadness. These were all the emotions I've felt over the past week, or at least the ones I can name. It had been six days since I got the call from Andres. I had barely eaten, and I refused to get out of bed. I slept all day, and my mind would race all night. I kept replaying the times I had spend with Avery in my head. I was desperately trying to remember a hint, or any kind of noticeable moment to realize she had been playing with my head this whole time. But there was none. I even took a leave from work because there was no way I would be able to focus. I hadn't left the house since that night. I had no motivation, I was numb. Avery came to the house when they got back, but I didn't answer the door. She stayed on the porch for 30 minutes, just waiting. She came back again that night. I let the phone go straight to voicemail each time she called. It was full of messages at this point. I chose not to listen to them. Ivan called one day too, probably to tell me the big news, but I didn't answer his call either. Last night was the first night I actually slept. I felt sick when I got out of bed, and I knew I needed to eat. After my shower I walked into the kitchen to try to find something to cook. I sigh as I opened the fridge. I forgot I hadn't been to the store since before I went to Ivan's. As I'm walking out of the kitchen, I hear a car pull up in the driveway. I peak out of the front window and see Lex's car. *What the hell.* I opened the front door as she was walking up the porch. She had two coffees and a bag of food in her hand. "Wow. You look like shit," she says as she walks up to me. She hands me a coffee and makes her way inside. I watch her as she looks around the living room and the kitchen, she looks confused as she sits down.

"Looking for something in particular?" I ask, taking a seat at the table. "What?" she asks.

"I watched you scan the house when you walked in," I say. She furrows her eyebrows.

"I just haven't been here in a while. You've changed it up in here," she says. *Nice save.* "Anyway, I brought food. I thought we could have breakfast together." She pulls the food out of the bag and hands me a plate. I had so many questions, but the smell of the food takes a hold of me. Lex watches me while I eat. Normally this would irritate me, but I was so hungry. When we finished, I grab our plates from the table and throw them away. I waited a few minutes for my food to settle and began the interrogation.

"Thanks for breakfast," I say and take a sip of my coffee.

"Oh, of course. It's been a couple of weeks, I figured we could have breakfast and catch up," she says. I nod my head.

"How did you know I was home?" I ask. She looks at me nervously.

"What do you mean?" "It's a weekday Lex. How did you know I would be home and not at work?" I ask. She stays quiet.

"Does it have anything to do with why you came in scanning the house?"

"Chloe…" she says.

"Why are you here Lex?" I could feel myself becoming frustrated.

"Avery reached out to Sara," she says.

"I don't want to know anything," I say quickly.

"She just wants to know you're okay," she says softly. I snapped at her.

"Look, I can't tell you what to do, but I will ask that you not mention this to Sara. Tell her I wasn't here or something. If I wanted Avery to know what was going on, I'd answer her calls." Her eyes widened, and I felt bad.

"If I promise not to say anything, will you tell me what happened?" she asks just I was getting up from the table. I turn to look at her, "Wait, you don't know?" I ask.

She shakes her head. "No one knows what's going on Chloe," she says. *Did Avery not recognize Andres at the restaurant? What if she really doesn't know what's going on? What if it was more of a statement than a proposal?*

"Chloe?" Lex says.

"Sorry, I…" I pause.

"We don't have to talk about it," she says. "I think I fucked up."

We spend the next hour or so talking about everything that has happened. Lex sat there quietly, letting me finish and I could tell she was full of questions.

"So, you told her to go?" she asks, confused. "I didn't say that," I say.

"But you didn't tell her to stay. I mean, not until she was gone," she said. I just stared at her.

"I'm sorry." "I just wanted it to be her decision. Everything's happening so fast for us," I say, and she cuts me off.

"You can't stop a love like the one the two of you have. Your souls are…the same. You can fight it all you want to, but it will never go away," she said. I rest my head in my hands.

"Even if you're right, it's already too late," I say. "You don't know that he actually proposed. Andres was simply just saying what he heard. Like you said, her boyfriend has been worried about her pulling away. You don't know the whole conversation," she said. She had a point. I jumped to conclusions without even giving Avery a chance. I still couldn't convince myself that it wasn't a proposal. We didn't talk the whole time she was there.

"She came to your house Chloe, and she's been calling Sara," she said. "I can't do it. I can't let myself believe that's not what happened, because what if it did." Lex's phone began to ring. "It's Sara," she said.

"You should go. I don't want to think about this anymore," I say. She gets up from the table and walks towards the front door. She looks back at me right before she leaves.

"You should call her."

I stay at the table for a while after Lex leaves. A part of me did want to call Avery, but I couldn't shake the feeling of it all being real. If the proposal didn't happen, would she still stay? *She said she would leave him, for us. If there was no us, would she choose to stay with him? She's probably going crazy right now. I let out a sigh. If it's not real and I've abandoned her because of my own insecurities, I'd never be able to forgive myself.* I was starting to feel sick again, so I went into my room to lay down. I checked my phone and saw a text from Lex.

"I told Sara I went by, but you didn't answer the door. She said she'd let Avery know. Chloe, I've never seen you like this before. Please don't beat yourself up about it. Call if you need anything." I put my phone down and went back to bed. When I start to wake up, I force myself to get out of bed and get dressed. I needed to go to the store. Even though I didn't get out of bed for days, my house needed to be cleaned and I needed groceries. I attempt to make myself look somewhat presentable, grab my keys and head out. A note fell on the porch when I opened the front door. I stare at it for a second before I kneel to grab it.

"Chloe, I'll be in town all weekend. Please call me. -Avery" I almost turn back around and walk inside, but I take a deep breath and get into my car. I was almost at the register when I ran into Sara.

"Chloe, hi," she says.

"Hey Sara," I say. We stand here awkwardly. She doesn't know I saw Lex or that I know she's been talking to Avery.

"Grabbing stuff for dinner?" I ask, trying to break the silence.

"Oh, yeah," she says smiling, holding up her things.

"Have you eaten? You should come and have dinner with us. I could grab some wine." I think about it for a second, and then I think about the note.

"Thanks Sara, but I have plans already," I say, trying to lie my way out of it. She smiles at me.

"Well, I won't keep you any longer then. Have fun," she says. She probably thinks I had plans with Avery, but I lied because I thought if I agreed to dinner, she would tell her I was there. I got home and put up the groceries, but I didn't want to be home. I couldn't call Lex, because I told Sara I had plans, so I decided to go out. I headed into my room to find an outfit. I settled for casual, but still nice. I stare at my reflection in the mirror after I finished getting ready. A few minutes later, I was out the door. I pull up a seat at the bar and order a drink. My hands were shaking and every time I heard the front door open, I would freeze. *I shouldn't have come out. What if she shows up*? I hear the bar stool next to me screech against the floor.

"You sure do clean up nice." I turn towards the sound of her voice.

"Lex, what the hell are you doing here?" I ask.

"I'll have whatever she's having," she tells the bartender.

"I thought I'd come have a drink." I laugh and shake my head. "So, should I chug this one to catch up? What number are you on?" she asks. I turn to face her again.

"It's my first," I say, lifting my glass. She raises her eyebrows. "Ask the bartender," I say, defensively. I think about the way she looked around the house when she came by earlier.

"Unbelievable," I say.

"What?" she asks.

"You're checking to see if I'm drunk. And earlier when you came by, you were looking around the house for evidence that I'd been drinking," I say.

"Chloe," she says.

"Don't," I say. I throw a twenty on the counter and grab my things.

"For the record, this is the first drink I've had since I got the call. Go ahead and relay the message." I feel the cool air hit me as I walk outside, and I can finally breathe.

"Chloe!" I hear from across the parking lot, but I don't look back to see who it is. I got in my car and sped away. I was so pissed at Lex. I know she means well, but she should be on my side. Not sneaking sound to give updates to Avery. *It was her. It was her voice I heard coming from the parking lot.* I should have known that would happen. Telling Sara I had plans was a mistake. Lex knew exactly where to find me. I drive around for a while. I knew if I went straight home that one of them would show up.

I was exhausted when I woke up the next morning. I forced myself, yet again, to get out of bed. I couldn't keep doing this, I couldn't keep mopping around. She went on the trip because I didn't ask her to stay. I needed to start holding myself accountable for the choices I had made. After my shower, I make myself some coffee and decide to clean the house. I played some music and started in the living room. All the Christmas decorations were still up, so I grab a box and put them away. Once I place the box in the attic, I begin to dust the furniture. The kitchen was not as bad to clean. I didn't have groceries, so there were hardly any dishes to wash. It felt good to be moving around. Lying in bed all day was only making things worse. By lunchtime I had cleaned the whole house. I had worked up an appetite, so I went into the kitchen and tried to figure out what to make. I started to think about Lex. I was so ugly to her yesterday. I pushed her away because I was hurting. I took her caring as betrayal and was starting to regret it. I grabbed my phone and began to type out a message. "Lex, I'm sorry. I was out of line yesterday. I couldn't see past the hurt. Thank you for checking on me, even though I was being an ass. It means a lot." I hit send. I make my plate, grab water, and sit down at the table. I was just about done when my phone started to ring.

"Hello," I say.

"Make me dinner and I'll forgive you," I hear Lex say. I laugh. "Bring wine and you got a deal. Oh, and bring Sara too," I say. She stays quiet.

"Are you sure?" she asks.

"Positive. Lex, I'm okay. I can't keep wallowing in my own self-pity. I've done enough of that already," I say. I heard her laugh.

"Thank God. That was getting hard to watch," she says jokingly. "Seriously, you saw me one day," I say back to her, and we both laugh. "Okay, how about we go by around seven?" she asks.

"Great. See you tonight," I say, and we hang up. I finish my lunch and clean up the kitchen again. I felt good but cleaning all morning had me kind of tired. Lunch also didn't help, so I grabbed a small blanket and relaxed on the couch. I turn on the T.V. for background noise and close my eyes.

"Chloe. Chloe, wake up." I open my eyes and see Avery sitting next to me on the couch.

"What are you doing here?" I ask sleepily. She caresses my face with her hand. I felt an overwhelming sense of peace.

"The front door was open. Sorry, I just let myself in," she says. I stared at her, still in disbelief that she was here.

"I had to see you. I had to know you were okay. I love you, Chloe." I reach for her hand and open my eyes.

"Avery?" I say. It felt so real. I thought she was actually here. I turn my head towards the front door. It was locked. I caught myself looking around, trying to find something to prove that it wasn't just a dream. *It could be more than just a dream.* I think about calling her and inviting her over for dinner. *Oh shit, dinner. What time is it?* I looked over at the clock and saw that it was almost five. I jump off the couch and take a shower before I start cooking. I stand in the kitchen thinking of what I could make for dinner. *Why not just make her favorite? It is an apology dinner after all.* I finished getting the salad ready and ran into my room to change. I don't get overly dressed since it's just Lex and Sara, but I at least wanted to change out of sweats. I see headlights through the window and begin serving our plates.

"Mmm," I hear Lex as her and Sara walk through the door. They come into the kitchen and Lex runs straight to me. She hugs me, swaying me side to side.

"Can you apologize to me more often?" she teases.

"Chloe makes the best chicken spaghetti," she tells Sara. I notice she's been watching me since they walked in. We saw each other at the store the other day, but it was brief. I'm sure Lex told her about the other night. She's probably wondering how I look so put together.

"Shall we?" I ask and we all take a seat at the table. Sara and I watch as Lex slowly savors her food.

"I made extra for you to take home, quit eating like that," I say, and Sara and I start laughing. Lex giggles and looks at both of us. "I'm sorry. It's so good," she says. We continued talking and I noticed that Sara had been texting the whole time. I was becoming paranoid. This was not how I wanted to spend my evening.

"More wine?" Sara asks and walks over to the counter to grab the bottle.

"Is she still talking to Avery?" I whisper to Lex once Sara gets up. She nods her head and looks down at her plate. I suddenly become both nervous and agitated. I take a sip of my wine and Sara comes and refills our glasses. There was an awkward silence as Sara sat back down. She looks at her phone again and I watch as he types a message. "Is it her?" I ask and both Lex and Sara look over at me.

"Is it Avery?" I ask, pointing at her phone. She looks over at Lex. *I shouldn't have asked. I just made it more awkward than it already was.* "Uhm, yeah. It's her," Sara says quietly. I nod my head and take another sip of my wine.

"She just wants to know you're okay Chloe," Sara says. I don't say anything, but I can feel Lex looking at me. "She was wondering if maybe she…"

"No," I say cutting her off. "Actually, it's getting late. We should call it a night," I say as I get up from the table and walk away.

"Chloe, I really am sorry about tonight. Sara's just trying to be a friend to Avery. I'm sure you can understand. Please don't be upset. Let us make it up to you. Let me know." I read when I woke up the next morning. I did understand. I've always wished Avery had someone to talk to, I just didn't think it would be Sara. It made sense though, that she would pick her. We all went on the trip together, and she was with

Lex. I just hate that they have to talk about what's going on, instead of something exciting.

"Don't apologize. I got nervous and overreacted. I feel so much better, but I'm not ready to see or talk to Avery. I hope Sara can not only understand, but respect that as well." I hit send and set my phone back down. I needed to get up and clean the kitchen. After Lex and Sara left, I went straight to bed. I was finishing up in the kitchen when I heard my phone ringing in the room.

"Hey Lex," I say as I answer the phone.

"Hey! Are you up?" she asks.

"Yeah, I was cleaning. What's up?" I ask.

"Was thinking brunch and mimosas. What do you think?" she asks. She sounded excited and it made me smile.

"Give me twenty minutes?" I ask.

"Okay, great! See you soon," she says, and I hang up. *Okay, let's try this again.* I walk into my room and throw on some jeans and a sweater. Just in case Lex wants to get a little crazy and pick a table outside. I let my hair down and did some light makeup. Lex is sitting at a table by the back door when I arrive. She's alone? She smiles and waves when she sees me walking towards her.

"Hi!" she says as I sit down.

"I ordered your food and drink already." I laugh.

"You're in a good mood. Where's your other half?" I ask and watch her smile fade.

"Oh, she's with Avery," she says and stares out of the window. "Lex," I say. She doesn't look at me.

"Hey," I say as I reach across the table to grab her hand. She looks up and gives me a guilty look.

"It's okay, Lex. Really. I'm glad she's with Sara. Honestly, it makes me feel better that she's not alone." I let go of her hand and she looks at me confused. *Of course she's confused. I damn near ran her and Sara off last night, and now I'm glad they're hanging out.* I let out a small laugh.

"I thought about it last night and this morning. The night we got back from the rip I asked her if it bothered her that she didn't have anyone to talk to about us. Now she does. It may not be the same right now, but I'm glad she has her." She smiled at me and raised her glass. "It's good to have you back Chloe," she says.

I flashed her a smile. "I'll cheers to that," I say and raise my glass to hers. "Okay, let's eat!" she says. We spent the next hour or so talking about what they did over the holidays. Sara went home to see her family for Christmas but was back in time to spend New Years Eve with Lex. She said they stayed in and had drinks. "I tried calling you, but you never answered. I figured you were with Avery," she says, taking a sip of her mimosa. "I sit there quietly, trying to put my days after the call together, but it was all a little hazy. "Chloe," she says, grabbing my attention. The waiter was standing at the table.

"Did you want another round?"

"Oh, sure. If you're having one," I say. The waiter nods his head and walks away.

"Sorry. I've been trying to put my days together. I can't fully remember them," I say embarrassingly.

"You've suppressed them. It was too painful at the moment and it's still too fresh. It's your mind protecting you," she says. *Would the memories come flooding back? God, I hope not.*

"I have a great idea," Lex says smiling as we wait for the bill. "We should spend the rest of the day eating snacks and watching movies." I look at her and laugh.

"Lex, are you drunk?" I ask and her smile fades.

"No. I'm not drunk. I do feel good though," she says smiling. "Come on. It'll be fun." I really didn't want to be alone. Keeping myself busy has helped so far.

"Your house or mine?" I ask. "I think yours would be better," she says. *Oh right. Sara's with Avery.* Lex pays for the food, and I pay for our drinks. We agreed to meet at my house. We walk through the front door, and just as I begin to tell Lex that we had forgotten the snacks, I stop. My mind began to race, and my heart began to ache. I could hear Lex talking, but I couldn't make out what she was saying. *Why would she do this? Is this why she was hanging out with Sara? Is this why Lex called? She had to know it would only remind me of him.* "Ivan," I whisper. I don't even realize I've said his name out loud until I hear Lex say "Ivan? Who's Ivan?" I could feel my eyes begin to water, but it wasn't out of sadness. I was becoming angry. The more I stared at the fort and all the snacks, the angrier I became.

"Chloe, who's Ivan?" Lex asks again. "Get out," I say. We're still standing at the front door.

"What?" Lex asks. I could hear the shock in her voice.

"Just leave!" I say.

"No!" she yells back at me.

"I'm not leaving." She shuts the front door and walks past me. She starts taking down the fort, throwing the extra blankets on the couch and grabbing the snacks from the floor.

"Lex, what are you doing?" I ask. "Taking this thing down," she says, not looking at me.

"It's obviously upsetting you, but I'm not going to let it ruin our movie day. Now come sit down." I walk over to the couch and sit.

"I'm sorry. I overheard them discussing it last night. I told Sara I knew where you kept a spare key. I thought it would be a good thing for you. I didn't know you would be triggered by it," she says. I take a deep breath, trying to calm myself.

"It's fine. Like you said, you didn't know," I say. I look over at her and smile.

"Throw me some of those snacks. What movie are we watching first?" she asks. Halfway through the movie, Lex gets up and walks to the kitchen. I can hear her talking but can't quite make out what she's saying. I get up quietly and walk to the entrance of the kitchen. I don't walk all the way in, but I got close enough to try to hear her.

"No. No Sara, she was pissed," I heard her say. She's quiet again. "She didn't say anything. All she said was 'Ivan' and I don't know who that is." More silence.

"I don't know. I'll be home tonight." I turn and walk back to the couch. The day Lex showed up with breakfast was the day I told her Avery was in a relationship. That, of course, was no surprise. I mentioned that they had been together for a couple of years, and that was the reason the proposal worried me. She didn't know who Ivan was. She didn't know Ivan was my best friend. More importantly, she didn't know Ivan was Avery's boyfriend. *I wonder if Sara knows. No, she couldn't. She would have already told Lex. That would mean Avery would have to explain why I wasn't talking to her, and still, no one knew what was going on.* "Is everything okay?" I ask Lex as she walks back into the room. "Oh, yeah. It was my mom," she says. She turned her attention back to the movie. She lied. We continue to watch the movie, but I don't pay much attention to it. *Should I tell Lex about Ivan? I wonder what she would think. Would she agree with Andres? Or would she disagree completely?*

"Okay, your turn to pick a movie," Lex says, handing me the remote. I could barely pay attention to the first one, how was I going to sit through another movie? I scrolled through the list, trying to find something that looked halfway interesting.

"Or we could do something else?" Lex says. I turn to look at her. "Like talk maybe? About whoever Ivan is?" I shake my head.

"No. We're not touching that," I say. I get up from the couch and walk to the kitchen.

"Then can we talk about the fort?" she asks, trailing behind me. I think about it for a minute, then pull the bottle out of the cabin. "I'll make you a deal," I say, and she stares at the bottle. I figured at some point that Avery told Sara about the drinking. I mean, Lex practically searched my house and followed me to the bar the other night. She'd back off after this for sure.

"I'll tell you whatever you want to know, if you get drunk with me." She looks at me and gets up, grabbing her keys. I knew she wouldn't agree to it. She makes her way to the front door and turns back to look at me.

"Are you coming? We're going to need more than that bottle."

Lex and I stayed up all night talking. She called Sara about an hour into our conversation and told her she was going to stay the night. We had a few drinks, but we stopped after three or four. I wanted to be able to talk about it soberly and Lex wanted to be sober enough to understand it all. I started off telling her about my friendship with Ivan. I could tell there were a couple of times where she was trying to figure out how he fit into the whole story. I needed her to know just how close we were though. Ivan was not just some guy. I take a deep breath and finally say the words out loud.

"Ivan is Avery's boyfriend." The room fell silent. Lex looked like she just got the worst news of her life.

"Oh, Chloe…" she says softly. I stay quiet, letting her process everything. "That makes more sense now. You could possibly be losing two people." I nod my head.

"Two important people," I say. "When we were on our trip, Andres said something to me. He said if Ivan knew me the way Andres did, then he would understand." Lex thought about it for a second. "Can I ask you a question?" she asks.

"Let's say it was a proposal, and she said yes. Would you understand?" Her question stuns me.

"You're upset because you're not sure if it did happen. Why?"

"I know we had a fight, but she was supposed to come back to me. We were supposed to start the year together. I don't know what changed," I say.

"Don't you think Ivan would feel the same way?" she asks. "Him and Avery loved each other. Don't you think he'd be wondering what changed?" I can feel the ache in my chest again.

"You'd really sacrifice your own happiness to make sure he'd never have to go through that wouldn't you?"

She pauses for a second. "What about her happiness?" I looked up at her, shocked.

"What?" I ask. "What about Avery's happiness?" I shrug.

"I guess I figured she'd be happy either way," I say.

"Let me ask you something else," she says. I sit up in my chair. I didn't expect all this from Lex, but I listened anyway.

"When is the last time Ivan called or texted you? You've been so worried about how the whole situation would make him feel, yet you haven't seen him since you left that weekend. And you're still trying to think about the last time he reached out. Avery's calling almost every day though. Stopping by, waiting to see if you'll answer the door. Calling people to come check on you because she's worried. She's even staying with her parents this weekend in hopes that you might call her." I didn't know what to say.

"It's late," she says a few minutes later. She stands up and reaches for my hand. She pulls me in for a hug when I get up and we stay like that for a second. I pull away as I feel my eyes benign to water.

"There are clean sheets on the bed in the guest room. I'll grab you a blanket from the laundry room," I say. I walk away from her and take a deep breath. I grabbed some pajamas from my room for her to sleep in. "Here you go," I say when I walk in the room. She smiles at me and takes the clothes.

"Think about what I said Chloe. I'll see you in the morning." I returned the smile and headed into my room to lay down. I had been so focused on what this would do to me and Ivan, that I failed to think about Avery. I grab my phone and stare at the screen before I turn it on. I pull up Avery's messages and start typing.

"I'm not ready to explain, but I need you to know that I'm okay. I love you, Avery." I hit send and put my phone on the nightstand. I turned around and a few minutes later I had fallen asleep. When I woke up the next morning, I could hear laughter and Lex talking in the kitchen. I throw my hair up and head into the bathroom to wash up. "Wow, it smells great in here," I say when I walk into the kitchen. Sara was sitting at the table and Lex was at the stove. I walk over to the counter to pour a cup of coffee and join Sara at the table.

"Avery left this morning," Sara says cautiously. I could feel Lex staring at me.

"Oh," I say. I didn't check my phone this morning to see if she had responded. "She was happy that you texted her." I smiled at her and changed the subject.

"What are you making?" I say and turn my attention to Lex. "French toast," she says with a cheesy smile. They stayed for a while after breakfast. Sara cleaned up the kitchen while Lex and I sat in the living room and talked.

"So, how are you feeling?" Lex asks.

"I'm okay. I think I'm going to go back to work tomorrow," I say. She smiles.

"Thank you for last night. It was definitely an eye opener. I have a lot to think about now. Like how I'm going to fix all this." She laughs. "I think the two of you will be just fine.

I go back into my room to lay down after they leave. I think about everything Lex said last night. I was so caught up in the way Ivan would feel that I had lost focus on what was important. I leaned over and grabbed my phone off the nightstand. There was a text from Avery. I was so nervous to read it.

"I wish you would talk to me Chloe. I have no idea what's going on, and no one is saying anything. Are you having second thoughts about us? If it's because of the fight, I'm sorry! I respect that you're not ready to talk, but it's driving me crazy. I love you, Chloe. Please call soon." I put my phone back on the nightstand. I need more time to think. The following week at work was hectic. I had so much work to catch up on after being gone for the holidays, but I was glad that it kept my mind busy. Lex texted a few times throughout the week, trying to schedule lunches, but I continued to make excuses. I know her and Sara were probably waiting for updates. Especially if Avery and Sara were still talking. At the end of the month my boss had scheduled a meeting with us all. He explained that the firm would be expanding, and he had a partner that had graduated college and was opening a new firm in another town. We talked about what it would mean for us moving forward with promotions and different assignments we would be taking on. At the end of the meeting, he asked me and Tristan to stay for a minute. Once everyone else exited the meeting room he said he had a question for us.

"Tristan, with you being head of accounting here, I would like for you to take over at the new firm," he said. Tristan looked over at me and then back at our boss.

"And Chloe," he continued. "You're one of the best secretary's I've had. I'd like you to go as well. You would be a big help while the new attorney settles in, and you would be able to train the team he puts together." *He wants me to move?* "How long are we talking about staying?" Tristan asks.

"Six months to a year," our boss says.

"Of course, if the city grows on you, you would be able to stay permanently." Tristan leans back in his seat and lets out a deep breath.

"Same goes for you Chloe." I immediately thought about Avery. *Would she come with me? Would she wait if I said yes?*

"I'll give you a month to think it over. He'll be opening in March. That's all for now," he says. Tristan and I get up and head back to our offices. The receptionist meets me at my door.

"Chloe, there's a gentleman named Ivan here to see you." My heart stops. *What the hell.*

"Can you tell him I'm still in a meeting?" I ask.

"Yes ma'am," she says and walks away. *Why is he here? What if something was wrong*? I pulled my phone out of my desk, but there were no messages. I call Avery without thinking.

"Chloe, hi," she says when she answers.

"Where are you? Are you okay?" I ask frantically.

"What? Yes, I'm fine. I'm at work. What's going on?" She asks. "Then why did he… Nothing. Never mind. I have to get back to work," I say.

"Chloe, wait…" I hung up before she could finish. There was a knock at the door.

"Come in," I say, trying to slow my breathing. Tristan walks in and sits in one of the chairs.

"I was not expecting that," he says. I sit back in my chair and try to relax.

"Yeah, me either," I say. "I'm going to order take out. I might stay late tonight. Do you want anything?" he asks.

"Actually, yes. That's perfect. I was planning on staying too," I say. "Okay. Maybe we can talk about this whole move," he says. I smile and nod my head. I wait until he walks out to check my phone. There were messages from Lex, Ivan, and Avery.

"Dinner tonight?"-Lex. "Hey Chloe. I was in town and tried stopping at the office. They said you were in a meeting. I don't know what's going on, but I wish you would call. Maybe come and stay with us this weekend? Let me know."-Ivan.

"It was Ivan, wasn't it? He just called. I didn't tell him I talked to you. In case you're avoiding him like you're avoiding me. It was good to hear your voice Chloe, even if it was just for a second."-Avery. I text Lex back and let her know I'm staying late and put my phone back in my desk. I finish up the file I'm working on and half an hour later Tristan comes in with our dinner.

"So, what do you thinking about the new job?" he asks when we're done eating.

"It's a lot to take in," I say.

"Yeah. It could be exciting though. Like a fresh start. I wouldn't mind a break from this place," he says. *I wouldn't either. Plus, if Avery and I took time to work things out, we could move. It could really be a fresh start.*

"Well, we have a month to think about it," he says. "It's getting late. We should call it a night." We pack up our things and go our separate ways. I go straight home from work. After I settle in, I pour myself a glass of wine and sit on the couch. *I wonder what Ivan was doing in town, without Avery. Why would he stop by the office? That wasn't like him.* Lex called after a while, and I let her know she can come by.

"You've been busy," she says, giving me a questionable look as she takes sip of her wine.

"Who knew taking a leave from work would have me so behind," I say sarcastically.

"Speaking of work…," I say, readjusting myself on the couch to face her.

"My boss offered me a position at a new law firm he's opening up," I say.

"Okay…" she says, waiting for more.

"There's a new attorney he's partnering with, fresh out of college. He wants me to help him start up and train the team he puts together," I say.

"That's great Chloe! Congratulations," she says excitingly. "It's in another city," I say and her jaw drops.

"I'd be there six months to a year. Depending on how quickly he gets up and running." She stays quiet for a minute.

"So, you would be moving?" she asks.

"If I say yes. Permanently if I like it. I have a month to decide," I say.

"A month?" she exclaims?

"What about your house? Your friends?" *Meaning her of course.* "What about Avery? Chloe… You are going to tell her, right?" she asks. I take another sip of my wine.

"I mean, yeah. I'd have to, but what if she doesn't want to go? I can't ask her to wait for me," I say.

"You can't make that decision for her," she says.

"Do you want to go?" I had thought about it all day. It would be great for my career, and the thought of the move was kind of exciting. I didn't want to be here forever.

"Yes," I say smiling.

"It could be really good Lex. I could keep the house, that way I'd always have a home to come back to..."

"Wait," she says cutting me off. "You're thinking about actually moving?" she asks. I can hear how upset she is in her voice.

"I'm good at my job Lex. I could really excel in a bigger city," I say. She leans back on the couch. *I thought she would be happier for me.*

"You could always come visit," I say smiling. "I know I'm pouting right now, but I'm happy for you," she says.

"Could you maybe not mention it to Sara?" I ask. "Chloe…," she says.

"Look, if Avery's going to hear about it, it should at least be from me," I say. She looks up at me.

"So, you're going to tell her?" she asks again.

"Yes Lex. When I decide," I say, and she smiles. "Ooh, can we have like a dinner party? You can let out the news then. It will be fun! I'll even act surprised," she says, and I laugh. "I think it's better if I tell Avery when we're alone," I say. She leans back on the couch again. "I just don't think throwing news like that at her at a party would end well," I say. She thinks about it for a second.

"Yeah, you're right. Sorry I got carried away. It could be the wine," she says, and we laugh.

It was mid-February when our boss called me and Tristan into his office.

"Well, what are your thoughts?" he asks. Tristan looks over at me and then back to him.

"I would love the opportunity," he says. They both looked towards me. I hesitate for a second.

"I would like to go as well, sir," I say. He stands up from his desk.

"Perfect! I'm very proud of all the hard work the two of you have put into this firm. I know you'll both do great," he says and walks around the desk to shake our hands.

"I'll send out the details in an email. You leave at the end of the month. Why don't we have lunch and celebrate? We can inform the rest of the team," he says. We headed back to our offices, and I sent Lex a message.

"It's official. I leave at the end of the month." I finished up my workday and headed to the store to grab some boxes. I had two weeks to pack and get things ready for the move. I also had to find time to tell Avery. *It would have to be this weekend. I need to give her enough time to think. She doesn't have to come when I leave. She would still need to tell her job, and Ivan. I still need to find a house. I should have thought this through better.* I send Lex a text, asking her to come by.

"I need you to get on my laptop and look for houses for me while I start trying to pack," I say when she walks in.

"Good think I brought this," she says holding up a bottle of wine. I smiled and ran to the kitchen to grab two glasses. After about an hour of house searching, and not enough packing, we agreed on one. It was a nice two-bedroom, two bathroom and had a beautiful backyard.

"I'm sure Avery would love it too," she says, nudging my shoulder.

"I'm telling her this weekend," I say.

"Really?" she asks. I nod my head and she leans over and hugs me.

"She's going to say yes Chloe." I smile. I hope so. I spent the rest of the week packing and calling the realtor to settle things with the house. I leave work early on Friday to clean up a bit before calling Avery to ask if she'd come over for the weekend. There was an envelope sticking out of the door when I drove up.

"Chloe" was all it said on the front, and I take it inside. I set my things on the table and opened the envelope. A letter falls out.

"Chloe, my best friend. I tried to give you this in person the other day. That's why I stopped by your office. It's also why we've been trying to get a hold of you since we got back from our trip. Over the past several years you've been the closest person to me, until I met her. I can't picture my life without her anymore. So, while we were away on our trip, I asked her to marry me. Chloe, she said yes! I can't do this day without you there. So, with his letter, I ask you. Will you be my best woman?"

I sink down to the chair at the table, hot tears rolling down my face. I couldn't breathe. There was an intense pain in my chest. I got up and threw the letter on the floor. I pull the bottle of whiskey out of the cabinet and stare at it before taking a drink. Memories of Avery and I ran through my mind. *She was supposed to come back to me.* I picked the letter up off the floor and read it repeatedly as I continued to drink. I let out a slight laugh as my thoughts begin to haunt me. My reasoning for never falling in love with a woman was finally coming true. I knew karma would come to collect the debt I owed for the pain I had caused. But none of that matters. She was gone and I am still me. I got up from the table and stumbled to find my phone. The phone rang as I patiently waited for her to answer.

"Chloe, hi," she says in the soft familiar voice I was used to. "Can you come, please?" I ask, trying not to sound as drunk as I felt. "Of course. I'll be right there." A few minutes later I heard a knock at the door. I take a deep breath as I reach for the doorknob. I pulled the door open, and tears began to fill my eyes again.

"Oh, Chloe. I'm glad you called." It was HER.

Milton Keynes UK
Ingram Content Group UK Ltd.
UKHW051853281024
450367UK00019B/285